The
PARALLEL
LIVES *of*
ELIZABETH ANN

The
PARALLEL
LIVES *of*
ELIZABETH ANN

Volume One: The Elizabeth Ann Trilogy

J. NICHOLS MOWERY

THE PARALLEL LIVES OF ELIZABETH ANN
Volume One: The Elizabeth Ann Trilogy

iUniverse books may be ordered through booksellers or by contacting:

iUniverse
1663 Liberty Drive
Bloomington, IN 47403
www.iuniverse.com
1-800-Authors (1-800-288-4677)

ISBN: 978-1-4917-5407-8 (sc)
ISBN: 978-1-4917-5408-5 (e)

Library of Congress Control Number: 2014922210

Printed in the United States of America.

iUniverse rev. date: 12/17/2014

CONTENTS

PROLOGUE

James Anderson's Cabin

Washington State's northern coastline was known to be wide open to harsh winter storms coming off the Pacific Ocean. However, due to these same wind patterns, Redcliff's Beach had more sunshine during the summer months than surrounding beaches. It was this fact which James Anderson used to explain his purchase of the five acre plot along Redcliff's Beach's northern frontage to his wife, Jill, a week after the birth of their first child, a daughter they named Dana Marie. Still feeling the twinges of childbirth, Jill smiled patiently as James excitedly explained his plans for a cabin of his dreams.

Though most of the five acres James chose was heavily wooded, it had a massive outcropping of an eon hardened basalt flow which sloped gently down to the beach in the exact middle of his acreage. It was on this solid stone outcropping which James intended to build his cabin.

When he first began, he drilled holes into the basalt in rows of 12, front to back, and set lengths of iron rebar into each hole so the rebar poked to the top of a framework he then built around the fifty-five by seventy-five foot base. This area would become the floor of the cabin. Cement was then mixed on site and the concrete was poured into the framework until it covered the tops of the rebar rods. When the last pour of the concrete was made, James hired a concrete worker to smooth the surface to a sleek shine. This surface was to be the cabin's floor for all time.

The next steps were to carefully bolt twelve foot six by six cedar posts to the concrete base for the cabin's framework. Then trusses for the roof went onto that framework and towered over the massive basalt to which it was attached. Toward the end of the two years it took to build this seaworthy cabin, word reached other beaches about Anderson's cabin and people hiked up the beach from the public parking to take pictures, watch him work or ask questions. Though James was proud of their keen interest, he seldom stopped for more than a few words as the deadline for the finished cabin was nearing and he needed every minute to finish before the birth of his second child, Elizabeth Ann.

During the final months, he built most of the cabin's interior as James was meticulous with details. Most of his effort centered on the yacht-style kitchen with its watertight cabinetry and food storage pantry. The placement of the wood cook stove was set next to the pantry along the south wall. The marble counter tops and the large country sink under the south window were the quality used in larger homes. Double faucets were added though only cold water would be available by gravity flow, from the water tower built high on the hill. It would be several years before a propane tank was brought in and hooked up to the hot water heater in the back of the pantry.

The water tower sat at the top of the driveway entrance, just off the newly paved road named Shoreline Drive which ended at the top of the north cliffs. The water tower could be easily reached by the tank truck bringing the fresh water. James signed a long term contract to have the tank refilled whenever he called to say when the family would arrive. The bathroom and kitchen were both plumbed to have running water. The toilet which James bought was a composting unit from Sweden. Hot water faucets, though installed, would not be of use until the propane water heater was connected in the future. However, enameled boilers sat on the wood stove ready to heat water to use for dishes and bathes.

James wanted the cabin to be as near perfect as he could make it before he brought Jill and the children out for the first time. With that in mind, he shopped for and purchased all necessities needed to set up a home. On the day the load of items was delivered, he placed each piece where it would have optimum use. A long leather sofa with two matching armchairs were set around a colorful Turkish rug spread over the gleaming concrete floor in front of the native stone fireplace built into the north wall with each stone collected by James from the mountains across Shoreline Drive.

A twelve foot black walnut farm table with its six matching chairs was found in an antique shop in Astoria and centered in front of the bank of windows next to the beachside glass slider door. A wide bench sat directly under those windows and was covered with thick seating pads and pillows to lean back against. James made certain a row of coat hooks along the north wall, close to the slider door, was there for the needed jackets and a box below was for wet sand covered boots and shoes.

James filled the kitchen cupboards with dishes, utensils, pots and pans and set four stools under the deep counter which enclosed the kitchen's workspace. In the bedroom, he set the head of the large bed at the east wall with the two chests of drawers under the south window. Two large cribs sat along the inside wall. Even the bathroom's cabinet storage was filled with supplies of towels, soap and tissue. Before he left for home that night, he went into to the bedroom and smiled as he imagined his children sleeping in their cribs. Seeing a wrinkle along the edge of one crib's quilt, James pulled it smooth and decided his cabin was ready for his family to enjoy.

On the morning they were to go to Redcliff's Beach, Jill carried two week old Elizabeth Ann, and the diaper bag, out to the car and tucked the baby into the seat behind hers. Two year old Dana Marie ran to her father's open arms and squealed when he swung her up over his head. Jill smiled as she tucked pillows and blankets around the infant and James settled Dana Marie into the seat beside the baby. Then more bedding was tucked around both for safety.

Though Jill noticed a utility trailer was hitched to the back of their car, she did not ask about it as she could tell, by the grin on her husband's face, it was to be a surprise. Quickly checking both children once more, she got into the car and James drove them away from their home in Hood River, Oregon.

An hour and a half later, he drove through the small community of Redcliff's Beach and, when they reached the cabin's driveway, turned off Shoreline Drive. At once, Jill saw the water tower hovering at the edge of the wooded five acres. However, the drive went around two more curves before those same woods opened to show the cabin built upon the massive basalt flow and opened the view to the beach. It was then that Jill saw an exquisite cabin standing proudly against an azure sky.

"James, oh, James, your cabin is so beautiful." She told him and, indeed, it was. The copper clad roof was held high above the dark grey stained cedar siding set off by wide white trim around all the windows and doors. The combination of these finishes with the native stone of the fireplace's outside wall caused the cabin to seem as if it loomed larger than Jill knew it could possibly be. In fact, to her, the cabin seemed ready to sail out on the next high tide. For several minutes, the couple sat staring silently at the beauty James had created. Finally, she said with a nod, "The stone work on the fireplace is a showstopper, James. Bravo. It must be exquisite in the cabin."

Though the front entrance to the cabin was tucked along the south side of the cabin, away from winter storms, the way to it was easily seen by the wide eave and an intricate trellis over two welcoming steps onto a wide deck. This deck paused at the front door then narrowed to continue towards the beach. Here the deck swept out several feet out over the sand dunes and was edged with a continuous bench across the frontage.

On the north side of this deck, six wide steps led down to a path through high sea-grass covered sand dunes that led out to the incoming waves several hundred feet to the west.

James beamed as he led his family along the south deck, past the front door and on to the beachside deck. Stopping to stare at this wonderful home, Jill held tiny Elizabeth Ann wrapped snuggly in her blanket and James wrapped his arms around his wife and they both stared at the front of his cabin. The spell was broken when two year old Dana Marie began to jump and stamp her tiny feet across the deck trying to make as much noise as her feet could muster. James and Jill turned their attention to her dance of joy until the baby turned red faced and it became clear that a diaper change would be needed soon.

This sent James racing back to the car for the diaper bag and he returned to her by entering the cabin through its front door. Opening the slider door for Jill, he escorted her inside and called for Dana Marie to follow them into the cabin. Without a moment to spare, she lay tiny Elizabeth Ann on the surface of the long farm table and made the quick change to a clean diaper. While she did this and disposed of the soiled one, James went back and forth to the utility trailer unloading items he'd brought to finish making the cabin their home away from home.

When both were done with their chores, James walked his family to the front door to introduce them to the door knobs and locks, showing off his good work. Then, he toured them to doors of rooms and showed how the bathroom fixtures worked and how bedroom looked with its bed extending off the east wall. When Jill saw the two cribs along the inner wall, she laid sleeping Elizabeth Ann in the one nearest to the bed and set the diaper bag on one chest of drawers under the south window.

Seeing the baby sleeping in the crib, Dana Marie demanded to be lifted into the other crib. Then, James laid a soft wool blanket over each child. When, he and Jill returned to the kitchen area, he showed her each watertight cabinet and the efficient pantry. Thirsty, she ran the tap water into the kettle beside the large sink and set it on the stove. Then, she filled a glass with the clear water and drank it down as she looked out the south window. When she turned to James, he wiped tears from her cheeks and knew the cabin was exactly what she hoped it would be. Then he took the glass from her and filled it, finding it refreshing.

Lastly, James led Jill to the long table and sat her on the bench by the window and explained why the fireplace did not set next to the kitchen's wood stove, but had been built on the north side of the cabin. "The wood cook stove will heat this end of the room and needed a smaller chimney for efficient drafting and hotter flame to cook food. Putting the fireplace on the north wall seemed so logical."

He told her where each stones had been found and how he'd carried them down the hill. When enough were collected, he'd hired the best stonemason in the area. Jill could see James took great pride in the finished work and she walked across to the chimney. As she ran her hands over each of the large stones, she told him how enchanted she was by the results.

Smiling wickedly at James, she pulled him to her and kissed her husband as he'd never been kissed before. From her crib, Dana Marie could see them through the open bedroom door and demanded to be picked up. This they did, though after giving her hugs and kisses, they laid her back under the blanket for a longer nap as baby Elizabeth Ann was still asleep.

Once both children were, again, asleep, Jill used the next hour to begin making lunch. The first thing she did was to build a fire in the woodstove, both to heat the kettle and to take the chill from the rooms. After filling the kettle from the faucet, she set it on the stove to heat for tea and washing. Soon the long dining table was laid with plates, a platter of sandwiches, fruit and cookies, a small glasses of milk and cups of steaming tea. By then, James had emptied their suitcases into the chests of drawers, stored the fresh produce next to the canned goods in the pantry and started a fire in the fireplace, all done with a dancing Dana Marie's supervision.

The last item, which James took from the trailer, was a long low wagon with large thick wheels and a handle so long an adult could pull it without bending over. When Jill saw him pull it onto the beachside deck, she laughed at its odd look until James explained it was for their excursions on the beach. "I can pull both children, baskets of food and jugs of water, without getting a kink in my back. Coming back each day, it'll carry the treasures the girls will find on the beach and you'll use to decorate the railings and cabin." Laughing, Jill declared James a genius and hugged him.

Late in the afternoon, the water jug was filled and sandwiches and fruit laid in the picnic basket. James folded a thick quilt was laid in the bottom of the wagon bed and tucked baby Elizabeth Ann into it. Then he'd carried it down the steps and pulled over to the path through the sand dunes. When he reached the edge of the waves, Dana Marie climbed onto the front of the wagon and let her short legs dangle on either side of the long handle.

Later, as James pulled the loaded wagon along the outgoing tide, Dana Marie slipped off the wagon and ran ahead of her family. Surprised by her agility, both parents laughed but realized their oldest daughter was going to need closer watching then they'd supposed.

Since the wide beach was empty. James and Jill let Dana Marie run ahead of them as they hiked the mile of beach towards the high red cliffs which gave Redcliff's Beach its name. It was at this time, that James told Jill of the strange phenomenon he'd experienced when he'd first begun to work on the cabin.

"Just before dark, I laid my sleeping bag near the fire pit I'd built against the slope of the basalt and was lying back looking up at the brilliant stars. When my eyes got tired of looking upwards, I looked at the waves rolling onto the sand and followed them to the cliffs. It was then I noticed a bright light seemed below the horizon. As my eyes adjusted to the dark, I could see the light was actually on cliff face and very low. That night, I decided it was another camper's light and tucked myself into my sleeping bag as I had a heavy work load planned for the next day and a long drive home. I convinced myself that I needed sleep more than I needed to investigate the mysterious light. That could wait for another day.

"However, the next weekend I saw the light shining before the sunset. I usually worked till after dark using two lanterns and the full moon, but that night I had come to a good place to stop work and was eating my dinner when I saw the light was neither another camper nor a beachcomber. I decided to trek up there in the morning before I started the day's work.

"Early the next morning, over my cup of tea, my eyes latched onto the flickering glow. I set my mug next to the fire-pit and raced down the mile of beach. As I ran along the edge of the waves, I kept focused on the red cliffs and the light seemed to beckon just to me. When I got within fifty feet of the cliff base, I realized the glow came from a large translucent protruding stone, a melon sized agate. The stone had been exposed after a massive hunk of red granite had broken off the cliff face. As I climbed onto the granite slab and walked to the large translucent agate, it glowed brighter and brighter, as if there were a fire within it.

"At that time, the stone stuck out from the cliff face as if it had been jammed into a hole too small for its size. The protruding end of the agate glowed and, so intrigued me, that I put both hands on its large rounded surface. It felt warm to my touch and that surprised me very much. I started to pull away and when I did, the stone moved under my hands and a large chunk of the translucent stone came off. Luckily, I caught the heavy stone without dropping it, but I was dumfounded, absolutely dumfounded and could only stare at what I held in my hands. Finally, I moved off the granite slab so I could lay the huge hunk of agate on the sand. I sat looking at it for some time.

"The hunk of stone was rounded on one side and nearly flat on the other. It was at least two feet wide, three feet long and a foot thick. I picked it up and carried it in both of my arms, as if it were a precious child, back to the cabin site and put it into the trunk of my car. I was bewildered and wondered what I did to have that beautiful stone fall into my hands.

Every time I came, after that, I brought the stone from the car and placed it next to my sleeping bag in my tent. After my work was done, each day, I'd talk to the stone about what I was doing for you and the children and our life. I also repeatedly asked why I'd been chosen to receive it.

"Everything I'm telling you, Jill, is the absolute truth. One morning I awoke and knew that beautiful translucent stone was to be set into the concrete floor at a specific place and that is what I did with it. I didn't show it to you this morning as I wanted to tell you the facts first. Did you notice the rug under the dining table? No? Good. When we get back, I'll remove the rug off the stone and you can see it under the dining table. That placement wasn't my idea. The stone told me where and how to set it into the floor and that's the full truth

"Tonight you'll see how it glows even long after the sun sets. It's truly amazing, Jill, truly amazing. I know the stone wasn't in the cliff face before I bought the land as I'd walked to these cliffs many times before then. No, the granite slab had not yet broken off. That happened sometime after I bought the land. I believe the beautiful translucent stone was for me to find and place within our cabin, for us and our children.

"When we get to the cliffs, you'll see how the rest of the translucent stone still protrudes from the cliff face. Last week I saw some people trying to pry it out of the cliff face and yelled at them. However, the stone held itself to its spot and wasn't even chipped. For some reason, the agate has chosen our family to be the caretakers of this end of Redcliff's Beach.

"I'm determined to find a way to protect the agate left in the cliffs. I've been asking Washington State to consider making the north cliffs a State Park of some sort. Even though a park will bring more people to our beach, it will help protect the natural beauty of the cliffs for all time."

When the couple reaches the slab of granite at the base of the red cliffs, James parks the wagon and lifts Dana Marie onto the slab's surface. Before saying a word to James, Jill picks the baby out of the wagon, climbs onto the granite slab and goes to stand in front of the large protruding stone glowing within the cliff face. Staring at the stone for several seconds, Jill raises her hand and slaps at the stone and yells, "I declare this run is good and done."

At this, James erupts with laughter and carries Dana Marie to where her mother stands. Taking the child's small hand in his, he pats the stone and shouts, "I declare this run good and done."

Laughing, Jill hugs him and says, "I like the way you said it better than the way I did. Let's slap the stone together with our children and use your words,"

"Let's do it." James agrees and holding the tiny hands of each daughter the parents tap the stone and shout, "I declare this run good and done."

ONE

June 1—Liz

LIZ hears the airplane coming from behind her as she runs along the line of foam left by the last wave. As the plane's roar grows louder, she races up the beach as if trying to outrun her pursuer. Then, suddenly, she whirls around to face the single engine plane skimming over the surf and raises both hands high over her head. Inside the cockpit, her husband, Peter Day, tips the wings in a brief salute before turning the craft to the northeast and soars up over the Coastal Mountain Range, straight into the rising sun. Blowing kisses, Liz loves their early morning races which send Peter off to his company at Boeing Field in Seattle. Running her fingers through her short mop of prematurely white hair, Liz watches the plane disappear over the peaks and whispers, "Be safe, my love, take care."

Before resuming her run, Liz looks to the massive red cliffs a half mile north of her, then, facing south, she studies the five mile stretch of beach to the south cliffs. Lights twinkle on and off within the tourist facilities of that area of Redcliff's Beach. Turning back to the north cliffs, Liz sees her part of the beach is still empty. "Great, I'll have my run by myself for a change."

Running at her top speed, Liz is nearly at the red cliffs and pushing herself hard, determined to set a new personal record, when something slams into her from behind. The force is so great that she staggers sideways, rights herself, slips on a patch of pebbles and is unable to stop her fall. Landing first on both knees, Liz smacks down, directly onto her stomach and knocks the breath out of her. Lying face down with her hands and feet splayed out in an awkward position, she lies there for several minutes, stunned by what happened.

When she finally stirs, Liz struggles to her feet, groaning loudly and stands bent over, hands on hips, breathing deeply. Finally, when her legs feel secure enough to take a few tentative steps, she looks back to where she's sure another person had fallen, and yells, "What the hell were you doing that you hit me so hard? Why the hell don't you watch where you're going?"

However, there is no one behind her and she turns completely around to see where they could have landed. Much to her amazement, the beach is empty, no one is anywhere close to her nor where she'd been hit. A bit frightened by this fact, she asks, "What could have hit me hard enough to knock me down and not be there? How weird is this? I know something hit me on the right side of my back. I have the pain to prove it. Whatever it was had to be big. Damn, I wouldn't have stumbled over my own feet. I was hit and hit hard. My shoulders and knees hurt like hell."

Following her tracks back to where she'd felt the blow, Liz finds her own last running steps and, from there, her footprints skew from side to side then dig into the sand as she tried not to fall. Where those footprints end, her knee-prints show deep in the hard packed sand, then marks also show in the sand where she smacked onto the beach and laid prone. Looking back, she sees something odd and walks over to three deep footprints dug into the sand which come at a right angle to her own footprints. At the point of her impact, these steps end and the sand shows only her own footprints and fall, nothing more.

Unable to explain the prints or her fall, she stops trying to figure it out and limps the last few feet to the base of the north red cliffs and the giant slab of granite which had fallen off the cliff face two years before she was born. Climbing onto the rock slab, Liz crosses it and stands in front the translucent stone protruding from the cliff face. Sighing with relief at having reached it, Liz brushes sand off her scraped knees and elbows as she studies the oddly shaped stone. The agate's size, shape and color always makes her smile, as it looks as if it was jammed into a hole much too small for it. Raising her hand, she slaps at the stone and shouts, "I declare this run good and done!"

Then, as she does after every run, she presses her forehead to the stone's cool surface and thinks of her parents and sister, Dana. Today, their images fill her mind as they have since they were killed in the car accident, years ago. Her strongest memory of them is the last day they were together, here at their touchstone, and at Dad's cabin on their Redcliff's Beach. Liz and Dana had raced each other to slap the touchstone as they had done since they were small children.

Late that afternoon, the family headed back to their home in Seattle in the family car and only blocks from their home, a drunk driver crashed head-on into the family car. Liz was the lone survivor as she was asleep in the back seat. Everyone, including the drunk driver, were killed. Ever since that day, whenever Liz runs to the cliffs, Dana runs beside her and Liz lets her win every race.

Turning from her touchstone, Liz looks down the six miles of beach to the south cliffs and wonders again about what could have hit her so hard yet not be seen on the beach. Though lights in nearby homes and cabins flicker on and off, this end of the beach is empty. Shoreline Drive shows a string of taillights heading south as residents head to open their businesses within the tourist center of the south beach.

Within minutes, a strong easterly wind brings a thick blanket of fog out from the mountains, crosses the beach and sweeps it out to the far horizon of the Pacific Ocean. Leaning against the cliff face, Liz watches lights, far and near, disappear behind the grey. Sudden streaks of red and orange and pink cut through the thick grey to color the beach and the horizon. "Red in the morning, sailors take warning. If a storm is coming. I'd better get going as these bruised knees won't want to go fast."

As she moves to the edge of the slab, a bright flash blinds her for several seconds. As she waits for the flash-print to fade from her vision, she frowns, "Where the hell did that come from? The sun's not high enough to reach me. So what was it? Damn, things are too weird today. I need to go home, clean my bruised knees and take a nap."

As visibility is very limited by the fog, Liz follows the edge of the waves and lets her aching body set her pace. "This fog must have filled every canyon in those mountains. It's a good thing that Peter flies by instruments most of the time. Still, it must have been rather scary going through those canyons."

Checking her watch, Liz sees it's nearly nine. "Well, he'd have gotten there two hours ago. By now, he and Bob Drake are far over the Pacific on their way to Hong Kong."

At the thought of the men and their business partnership, Liz frowns. "Why do I have such doubts about those two guys going there for business? I'd love to go to Hong Kong but Peter never takes me up on it whenever I suggest I'd like to go with him. He just assures me I'd be bored and he'd be grumpy. This trip is for items needed for holiday shoppers. I'd love to get an early peak at the season and how the buys are made. They both insist the week is so filled with what is needed to see and buy that they must keep to their schedules. All I really know about their trips is their cellphone numbers and the date of their return flight, Those two great looking guys should never be let loose in a city known for its beautiful exotic women. This week it's Hong Kong and the next trip it's Amsterdam. Hell, those two could have a gal in every port for all I know.

"I know I shouldn't have grilled him with so many questions before he left this morning. It sure made him mad. When he said, 'Damn it, Liz, we have a good marriage. You've trusted me all these years as I've trusted you. I know you've been faithful to me and I've never done anything to cause you to doubt me. Why are you questioning me now? We have one of the best marriages of any couple we know.' Then he took me in his arms and gave me that long wonderful kiss and sent my head spinning. When we came up for air, I told him that I love him so much I'm sure every woman wants him as much as I do."

Answering her own doubts with a shake of her head, Liz limps along the waves until she hears the flap of a flag. Turning from the waves, she walks to the entrance to the path through the sand dunes to her home. There she looks up at the flagpole Peter put up years before. Smiling, she remembers how he'd told friends and family, 'it's so Liz won't miss the path to our home and end up in some other guy's bed.'

Chuckling at the memory, she follows the path to the steps to the deck of her home. When she sees the slider door is wide open, Liz is shocked as she's certain she locked it when she left. Cautiously walking up the steps, she goes to the door and looks inside. To her left, she sees the 'nine-iron' golf club leaning in the corner, left there for such scares. Grabbing it, she tiptoes past the dining table where the agate in the floor is pulsing with short bursts of light as if alarmed.

When she gets to the kitchen counter, Liz sees a dark shape in the hall next to Peter's office door. Raising the nine-iron above her head, she shouts, "Whoever you are, come out of there, right now."

When the shape stands up, Liz sees it's her neighbor, Alexandria Petrow, from next door. The woman steps out of the dark hallway, smiles broadly at Liz and walks directly to where she stands with the nine iron raised over her head. "Hello Liz. Glad you finally got home. You were gone so long I came over to check on you. Holy cow, you're a mess. What happened to you?"

Shaken, Liz frowns as she gives a brief explanation of what happened on her morning run. Then she catches herself and demands, "No, Alex, no. I'm the one doing the asking. How did you get into my home? I know I locked the slider door before I left. So how did you get in here? Didn't you hear me, Alex? I want to know how you got into my home.

"As for why I'm later, the fall and the fog. Now tell me, Alex, I'm angry and I want some explanation. Damn it. Too many odd things are happening today and I insist you tell me why you thought it was alright to break into my home when I'm not here. I don't like it one bit, not one bit. I would never go into your house when you weren't there. Never."

The smile on Alex's face fades and she stares silently at Liz. Then, she pulls herself to her full six foot height and glowers at Liz. It's this

Alex which Peter's description fits perfectly, 'a piece of raunchy Russian royalty with a bad vodka accent.' It's this Russian ballerina, who defected long before the breakup of the USSR, it is this Alexandria Petrow, she has never really seen before.

Walking defiantly past Liz, the woman goes out through the open door, then turns and snaps her fingers, "Hey Liz, lighten up, there's no problem. I needed my book Peter borrowed a month ago and came to get it. I was certain you wouldn't mind if I came in to look for it while you were on your run. I tried to check in his office but his door is locked. Do you have the key? I really need the book for my trip tomorrow."

Irritated, both by her injuries and the woman's attitude, Liz snarls, "No, Alex, I don't have a key to Peter's office. Even if I did, I would never open his office to anyone without his permission. I don't believe Peter would ever borrow anything from you. He doesn't like you and he doesn't want me to have anything to do with you. You know that. Don't deny it. Besides, you said you would be gone this week. Why did you come back?"

Ignoring Liz's questions, Alex says, "I waited on the deck for you to return from your run, Liz. I tried the slider door and it opened. You should be more careful as there are terrible people out and about. Besides, I wanted to tell you what I saw this morning. After Peter flew off you ran along the shore. When you were almost at the cliffs, someone came from behind and hit you very hard. It seemed to take you a long while to get up and walk to the rock.

"Then the fog came and you were gone so long, I got worried and came over to see it you'd gotten back without my noticing. I wanted to ask you to come for lunch as I've made up my mama's yummy pot stickers. How about it, Liz, do you have time for a good talk like old times?"

Still frowning, Liz shakes her head as she answers, "No, Alex. Not today. I need to shower and clean my scrapes and bruises from my fall. Please, go home. Now. Maybe I'll be over later. I want to rest after I shower and cleanup. I'll ask Peter about your book when he calls this evening. What did you say the title…?

"Hey, Alex, wait just a minute. You said you saw me fall on the beach after Peter flew off. Did you see who hit me? It was a terrible blow and I really took a tumble. My knees, hands and elbows still throb."

"Your run was wild as I see many changes coming at you. Peter has much change also. Do you see what I mean? Come to my house and I will tell you all that I saw." Alex grabs Liz's arm and tries to pull her out the slider door.

"Don't, Alex. " Liz snaps, pushing away. "I said I'm not coming over. I want a shower and a nap. Besides, you'll just prattle on and on about nothing. Why do you always try to get me to do things after I've said I don't want to do them? Just go, Alex. I want to bathe and rest."

Alex's smile crumples, "I did not mean to upset you, Liz."

"Go, Alex, leave. Now. I want a shower and nap. What's the name of that book? I'll ask Peter where he left it."

As if she doesn't hear Liz, Alex answers her earlier question. "You were hit by a woman who ran right through you. She was you only with long white hair tied back into a ponytail. Wham. She hit you and you both fell onto the sand."

For several seconds, Liz stares at Alex, then she begins to laugh, "Alex, why would you ever say that? There was no one on the beach with me this morning. No one. Not with me nor near me. Not anyone. Maybe there were after I started home. By that time, the fog was thick I could only see a foot in front of me. No, Alex, just go away. I don't want to hear another one of your long rambling stories Go home."

Alex's face softens, "You come to my house in the afternoon and we'll talk while I cook dinner. Alex loves to fix good food for good friends." Then, seeing the dark look on Liz's face, she walks out the slider door. "Remember, pot stickers don't taste good if they sit too long."

Watching Alex hurry up the path through the dunes, Liz mutters, "Thank God, I finally got the gumption to tell her to go away. She never answers any of my questions and I'm certain she won't today, whether at noon or later. I'm tired of getting the runaround from her."

Limping up the stairs to her bedroom, Liz thinks aloud, "Hell, if I'm honest, I got the same runaround from Peter this morning when I asked when he'd be back. Why do people answer questions with questions? I'm realizing I don't know anything about anything. Not about Peter nor Bob nor their business nor about Alex nor about her business. From now on, I'm demanding answers to my questions. When Peter gets home, I'm sitting him down at the table and he must tell me everything about everything. Right now, I'm feeling very stupid."

After her shower, Liz tucks herself into bed and falls into a deep welcoming sleep. When she awakens from her nap, it's late afternoon. Feeling a bit guilty, she calls Alex to apologize for missing her lunch and, to Liz's surprise, Alex tells her, "Not a problem, dear. Why don't you come over for dinner around six?" Pleased with the invite, Liz thanks her and goes to freshen her makeup and dress in better clothes, her former resolve and determination forgotten.

When ready, she goes out the front door and walks up the driveway to the trail which winds up through the wooded acres and ends at the edge of Alex's property. The lovely path is filled with childhood memories as Liz moves slowly through the thicket of manzanita shrubs, storm shaped shore pines and twisted firs.

Walking the trail has the same effect on Liz as her run to the cliffs does. The piece of woods was her father's gift to his family and, whenever she uses the trail, Liz feels her family close to her. At every turn, past every thick growth of brush, she feels their presence and gives thanks for having the wisdom to keep the acreage intact.

When she reaches the highest point on the trail, Liz stops to lean against the ancient shore pine and rest her bruised knees. This had been her sister's favorite spot as the view of the beach at that point is spectacular. Liz whispers, "Dana, I'm here, at your favorite place, where you'd sit in this old tree and watch the ocean for hours at a time."

A sudden breeze moves through the trees, bending the thinnest limbs and shaking a few of last year's cones from the firs. Sounds from the beach come with it and one louder voice penetrates Liz's daydreaming. Cocking her head, she is certain she hears her name being called. When, the tone changes, she is startled by the urgency of the voice. Ignoring the pain from her knees, Liz hurries back down the path to her driveway.

As she emerges from the high brush, she is shocked to see a patrol car parked in front of her garage.

A tall uniformed man is walking along the north deck tapping at each window, on that side of the house, calling out, "Mrs. Day, are you home, Mrs. Day?"

Frightened, Liz shouts at him, "Hey there. Hello? Can I help you? Are you looking for me? How can I help you?"

Hearing her voice, the deputy turns and sees her limping down the driveway. Hurrying to meet her, he takes her hand and asks, "Are you, Mrs. Day? I'm looking for Mrs. Peter Day. Would that be you?"

"Yes, I'm Peter Day's wife, Liz Day. How can I help you?" She pants the words, hoping he will not answer. More than anything else, Liz does not want to hear what this man has to say to her.

"Mrs. Day? Can we go inside your home before we talk? Please? Let me help you inside. Is this the best way?" As he speaks, he gently escorts her to the front door of her own home. "Can you open the door for us? Please? Let's go inside where we can talk privately."

Without answering, Liz unlocks the door and, once inside, rushes through her home to stand in front of the slider door and looks out at the ocean. The deputy steps up behind her and gently touches her arm. He is too gentle as he guides her to the closest chair, Peter's chair, and he is far too gentle when he eases her down into it.

Kneeling in front of Liz, the man speaks softly. "Mrs. Day, I have very bad news. Your husband's plane crashed this morning. It seems he flew too low in the fog and the plane crashed into the highest mountain north of here, Mt. Michael. Reports from witnesses say they heard a small plane having engine trouble, around six this morning. Reports said it was very low. That's all, just too low. Then the engine stopped and the plane crashed. We got several reports of the loud crash. However, due to the thick fog, it took most of the morning to locate the crash site. Luckily, the locator in his plane had turned on on impact. However, rescue crews had to go by foot as helicopters couldn't go up in that thick fog. They reached him around two this afternoon. He was alive but badly injured. They were able to remove him from the twisted wreckage of the plane. However, he died while being carried down the trail. They said he'd lost too much blood.

"Mrs. Day? Did you hear me? Mrs. Day? I'm sorry to have to tell you this. Your husband died from his wounds from the plane crash. The search party feels very badly they couldn't reach him in the morning. They told me to give you their condolences. Is there anything I can do for you, Mrs. Day? Anything I can get you? Is there anyone I can call? Mrs. Day? Who should I call to come here and stay with you? Mrs. Day?"

TWO

June 1—Beth

BETH sets her cereal bowl and coffee mug in the kitchen sink and runs water into them. Turning towards the hospital bed in front of the beachside windows, she watches the woman laying on it struggle for each shallow breath. As if trying to breathe for her, Beth takes deep breaths in time with those of the other. When a moan escapes the woman's lips, Beth frowns and thinks about cancelling her morning run. Bending over the bed, she kisses the cool brow and whispers, "That's right, my love, breathe, my darling Maxine, breathe, release, breathe, release."

Taking one cool hand in both of hers, Beth presses it to her lips and prays, "Please, Lord, let this be a good day, a day without pain, without fear. Let Max sleep undisturbed. Give her peace." Tucking the hand under the sheet, Beth makes her decision and whispers, "I'll be back soon, my love. I'm going for our run to the cliffs. Sleep. I'll be back soon."

Knowing not to expect an answer, Beth picks the hooded sweatshirt off the nearby chair, slips it on and goes out the slider door onto the beachside deck. As she closes the door behind her, she sees the glow from under the bed and knows her Dad's hunk of translucent agate is watching over her love. Blinking back the tears, Beth watches high rollers sweep across the flat beach as the first high tide of the day is nearing its peak.

Leaping off the deck, she runs the few yards across the flat sand to the edge of the waves and follows the line of foam to the north red cliffs. As if trying to outrun the ache in her heart, she focuses on a soft pulsing glow on the cliff face, a mile to the north. Running as if her life depended upon reaching the granite slab in record time, Beth races to their touchstone and to slap the stone one last time for Maxine.

Though Maxine is not with her, Beth feels her, matching stride for stride, as she pushes herself hard, leaving deep footprints in the sand. More than anything else, she wishes there were two sets of prints instead of only her own.

When her father built his cabin on the high basalt point, he built it to hold back the strongest storms. Beth was a baby when the family began spending summers and holidays at the beach. No matter what, the family was always sure their cabin would be waiting for them. In those first years, rows of other cabins, hotels and restaurants spread along the full length of Shoreline Drive, The curved beach held sea grass topped sand dunes hundreds of feet deep. Both ends of the beautiful beach were capped by high cliffs which protected Redcliff's Beach.

However, during the mid-century years, several destructive earthquakes hit the coastal areas. These, joined up with demon storms with massive waves, tore everything apart and carried it away. By the end of the century, her Dad's cabin, on its high basalt point, was the only structure which was still standing. The wooded acres were buried when the strong winds pushed the sand dunes off the beach and across to the other side of Shoreline Drive. Now, the least storm crashes onto the basalt point and licks at the cabin's underpinnings as the waves flatten the low dunes.

On this morning's run, Beth shares the beach with float logs wrapped with kelp and piles of debris rolling in on each high wave. When she is nearly to the granite slab at the base of the cliffs, a large float log is thrown onto the beach by a massive wave and it lands in front of Beth. The distance to it is short and she doesn't have time to change her direction, so she picks up speed and leaps over it with ease. Then she raises her arms over her head and yells, "Wahoo!" as she continues her run.

When she nears the granite slab, and running at her top speed, Beth slams full force into something unseen yet so solid she is thrown backwards onto the hard packed sand and knocked unconscious. After several minutes, cold water washes against her and she is pushed on to her right side by the incoming waves. When a large wave rolls her completely over as if she were a float log, Beth struggles onto her hands and knees, coughing and gagging. Crawling out of the wash of the seawater, she struggles upright then limps over to the granite slab at the base of the red cliffs and leans against the massive rock.

Wiping off her face, her hands come away covered with blood. Looking down, Beth sees fresh blood is dripping onto the front of her sweat jacket. Pinching her nose, she ignores the pain and holds onto it to stem the flow of the bleeding. After a minute, she carefully lets go and checks her hands for fresh bleeding. Seeing the flow has slowed, she carefully checks the rest of her body for any damage.

Feeling her legs under her, Beth walks into the waves and washes her hands and face with the cold water. The water refreshes her and she tries to think about what could have happened. "What did I run into? I didn't see anything in front of me. There wasn't anything on the beach except the float log I jumped over, I'm sure of that."

Looking to where she's collided, Beth sees there is nothing on the beach other than a bit of debris brought in by the last waves. There is nothing high enough nor long enough to have smashed her nose against. The largest log is a hundred feet down the beach and now resting at the high tide line.

Completely puzzled, Beth moves along the granite slab to where she can climb onto it. When she stands up, her head spins a bit as she goes to the cliff face and puts her hands on the protruding translucent agate that glows softly in the morning mist. Putting her forehead to it, she whispers, "I declare this run good and done." Though she pats the stone gently, instead of her usual slap, Beth feels pain surge down her left side. However, the worst pain is from her nose and she knows it's broken.

Beth begins to sob and she rages at the one thing which has changed her life so radically this past year, Maxine's ovarian cancer. The immanent loss of her loved one is more than she can endure and she shouts, "Give me back my life. I want days without worry, without pain. I want joy and laughter to ring through our home again. I want Maxine healthy again. I want our lives to do all over again. Do you hear me? Blast you. Whoever or whatever you are, do you hear me? Give back the love of my life or take her today. Don't make her endure one more second of that horrible pain."

Choking, Beth spits bloody mucus onto the sand, then blows her nose on the soaked sleeve of her jacket. Pounding her fists on the cliff face, she shouts, "Max wants to leave this life. I see death in her eyes every minute. She wants no more of this life yet you keep her here. Take her. I'll survive without her love or her laughter. Take her now, damn it. Give her peace."

Turning to the ocean, Beth sees a high wave sweep in from around the cliff point. Inside its movement, a bright pink flash winks at her. As the wave pools around the granite slab, Beth sees a large pink snail shell, directly below where she stands, resting against the granite slab.

Jumping into the flattened wave, she picks up the shell and stuffs it into her jacket pocket before she climbs back onto the granite. At that time, a series of waves sweep around the cliff point, one wave after another, each piling on and over the last, so when the waves hit the granite slab, Beth is swept up and over to the far side of the flat slab. In the moment before her inevitable fall, a brilliant light flashes into her eyes and blinds her. Then the rush of sea water pushes her off the granite slab and she falls onto the hard packed sand. When her knees hit the sand, she screams, "No, not again."

Shaken, both by the painful fall and the brilliant flash, Beth turns to yell at whoever pushed her off the rock and sees only a green flash print. "Why'd you push me? What did I ever do to you?" she yells, blinking to clear the flash print from her eyes.

When her eyes are clear again, she sees there is no one on the granite slab. Puzzled, Beth wonders why she'd been so sure someone had pushed her. Then she realizes the green flash print was the outline of a woman. Looking around the area, she sees the beach is empty except for herself.

As large waves continue to crash over the granite slab, Beth limps up to the base of the tall hollow ancient tree stump that has stood near the cliffs for as long as she's been alive. Knowing the tree trunk is the only thing left of a cedar forest that once covered the area when her father was a young man. Sitting slowly down on the deep dry sand, she leans back against it sun heated wood. Watching the sun burn off the morning mist, she lets sun's heat ease her aching body and dry her wave soaked clothing.

Soon, Beth's eyes close as images of her parents and sister, Dee, fill her mind and her thoughts take her back to the early years when her family picnicked beside this same ancient monolith. When she and Dee played house inside the hollow stump, the sand filled the trunk then and the short stump made a perfect shelter for two small girls playing with their dolls.

Years later, the sand inside the tall trunk has been sucked out of the hollow form by winds and waves and, now, the silvered monolith stands at its full weathered height. During those first years, their Dad told them about playing amongst a cedar grove that stretched hundreds of feet westward before it reached the waves. It was the loss of that forest, during the years of his youth, which caused their Dad to build on the basalt point, high off the beach.

Beth's daydreams are suddenly interrupted by two squabbling seagulls fighting over a dead fish brought in by the last wave. As they scream and flap their way to the top of the hollow stump, their sharp cries bring more gulls to their fight and Beth finds herself amongst flapping wings and snapping beaks.

Struggling onto her feet, she limps away, down the beach, as fast as she can go. When she stops to look back, she sees the birds are gone and the tide has peaked within a few feet of where she'd been sitting.

Stunned, she knows the turning of the tide means Maxine has been alone far too long and a rush of fear fills her with dread. Trying to run, she is slowed to a walk as pain shoots through her legs. Crying out, she pleads, "Please, let her be alive when I get home. Don't take her before I get there to be with her. Please, let what I left this morning, be there when I get home. Tell Maxine to wait for me."

Fighting against the pains shooting through her body, Beth tries again to understand what she smashed into, "Nothing was on the beach. Nothing." Thinking through the moment of the hard impact, she wonders, "Will I ever know what I hit this morning. Was there a person I didn't see? No, it wasn't that dark and where could they have gone so fast? If they'd been hit as much as I was, they'd be as injured as I am. Why didn't I see what was on my beach?"

At a large pile of debris, Beth sees a straight limb poking out of it and pulls it out. Using it as a cane, the support eases her pain and helps her move a bit faster. When she finally reaches her deck, she tries to brush the sand off her clothing and her hand hits the hard shell in her jacket pocket. Pulling it out, she studies it and whispers, "A perfect shell for my darling Maxine."

Opening the slider door, Beth waits next to it and holds her breath against the room's silence. Only when she sees Maxine breathe, so does she. Leaning over the bed, she whispers, "Maxine, sweetheart, I'm home. Look what I found for you. This shell came to me in a wave from around the end of the cliffs. Then it was left and I brought it home to you. See how large and bright pink it is? It's a perfect shell for my perfect Maxine."

Maxine's eyes open and she takes the shell Beth holds out to her. "Oh, Beth, So lovely. Where?" Her dark eyes widen as Beth tells of the pink shell rolling within the wave and when Beth finishes, Maxine says, "Beth, dear, I must leave you, I must go. The shell holds my love, always."

Choking back a sob, Beth answers, "I'll cherish it forever, my darling. I'll tell everyone it's a gift from the sea to the most beautiful woman that ever lived. My Maxine, my soul mate, my best friend, my love. Thank you for loving me for all these years. Max, thank you for bringing me joy." Beth forces a lightness in her voice until she sees Maxine close her eyes and again struggle to breathe.

Unable to hold onto her emotions one second longer, Beth says, "I release you, Maxine. Go to that better place, that place you go each day. Be finished with this life, with your pain. My darling, my Maxine, my love, find peace. I send you away with love. I will find a way to live without your laughter. Leave me, today."

As if an answer, Maxine opens her eyes and smiles, "Beth, darling, I sailed away, pink shell boat, found you, here as always." Unable to answer, Beth presses her lips to Maxine's forehead and lets her tears fall into Maxine's hair, not bothering to wipe them off. Taking the pink shell from the thin hand, Beth places it on the plate of shells sitting in the center of the dining table and sees the stone in the floor under the hospital bed is pulsing brightly.

Turning around, she goes out to the deck and strips off her wet sandy clothes and drapes them over the deck railing. Then she goes in to shower and dress in clean clothes. Afterwards, Beth wipes steam off the mirror and sees for the first time the swelling in the middle of her face. "Yup, my nose is broken. I should see my doctor. I will, just not today. Ice will help. I simply can't leave Max again. I'll go tomorrow."

Going to the kitchen, she heats a mug of leftover coffee in the microwave and carries to the side-table by Max's bed. As she reaches to set it down, she bumps it against the table's edge and the hot liquid splashes over her right hand. Shaking her hand in the air, she yelps, "Damn, that's hot!"

Rushing to the kitchen sink, Beth holds the reddening hand under the cold water tap. Suddenly, she erupts with laughter and turns towards the hospital bed. "Maxine, darling, remember how you demanded that whenever I had coffee, I should smack my lips and say 'Mmm-mmm, damn that's good coffee. Hot and black. Just as I like my women.' Whenever I did say it, you'd scream with laughter as you loved to see the shocked looks on other people's faces. Then you'd tell them that since the two of us were such strong powerful women, they had to know we could laugh at ourselves.

"And laugh we did, my darling. We rocked our world with laughter every day of our life together. Both of us lesbians, one ebony and one ivory, both with framed PhDs hanging on our walls. My darling, dearest Max, we were so full of ourselves that we didn't give a damn what others thought. Oh, dear heart, how amazing it was that our lives joined together for so many years. What a wonderful day it was when we declared our love to each other, right here on this beach, blessed by God, our families and friends. Each of us pledging our lives to the other. Oh, Max, what a miracle of love we have been. What a wonderful life we've lived."

Beth smiles as she turns off the cold water tap and pats her cooled hand dry. This time, she kisses Max on the cheek and goes out the slider door, leaving it wide open and the mug of cooling coffee forgotten on the side-table. Looking out at Redcliff's Beach, she sees the empty six miles of beach spread before her and she wishes for what she knows is impossible, a normal sister.

How wonderful it would be if Dee were still the sister she'd been before the drunk driver rammed Dad's car and not thrown into the windshield. She got that horrible concussion all because she wouldn't wear a seatbelt as it wrinkled her clothes. Stupid is as stupid does. Though she was the only one severely hurt in the crash, the changes in her head made life unbearable for everyone after that. From that moment on, Dee was a horrible person to everyone but especially to me. So much so, I've often wished she'd died that day. That day, I lost my best friend, my precious sister and got a devil named Dee.'

Years later, the sisters heard that their parents left the cabin and the land to both of them hoping the joint ownership would bring them close again. However, when Dee heard, she screamed she wanted to be cashed out as she would never share anything with that pair of queers.

As Beth and Maxine were used to Dee's remarks, they were not surprised by her decision. They gathered the money from several sources and paid Dee more than her fair share and making certain she relinquished all future claims. The courts ruled the sale, of the cabin with the five acres, was final and non-revocable.

That payment was twenty years ago, before Max's doctors said her cancer was terminal and had only six months to live. When Maxine told Beth she wanted to live at Redcliff's Beach for whatever time she had left. Beth took her sabbatical. For the first four of those months, the two women laughed and loved and lived a wonderful life,

Gradually the laughter stopped. By the first week of the sixth month, Beth knew Maxine was slipping away to some other place every time she stared at the ocean. That was when Beth decided to return the cabin and the land back to the State of Washington. Maxine was thrilled and, after talking it over with their lawyer, their offer was presented to Washington State Parks and accepted. The cabin and land became public property, 'a shoreline preserve with no future development or sale of land allowed for eons to come,' and renamed, 'The Maxine Oakley Preserve'.

Their lawyer added a line which allowed Beth or Maxine to use the cabin for as long as either lived. Though she was ill, Max went with Beth to sign the papers for the transfer and the action pleased everyone, except Dee McGowan.

When she heard the news, Dee did an about-face and demanded the State return the cabin's ownership to her twin daughters, Nicole and Nancy McGowan. The State's lawyers responded by sending copies of the sale and legal transfer to each family member and the family's lawyer. The State legislature quickly declared the land's transfer final.

That was when Dee turned her abuse acts to those around her. After several visits from the police, her husband, Dr. Ed McGowan, was required to sign Dee into his private sanitarium 'for several months of rest and treatment'. Frowning, Beth mutters, "Poor stupid woman, doesn't she realize I get use of the cabin until the sea washes it away or I die, whichever comes first."

A sudden movement, to her right, causes Beth to see a woman walk onto the deck, cross to a slider door and go into the house. She has shoulder length white hair and her resemblance to Beth causes Beth to gasp, "My god, who are you? We could be twins. Wait, don't go inside. Damn it, I said not to go inside. Stop. Tell me who you are."

Showing no reaction to Beth's demands, the woman shuts the slider door behind her and disappears. Beth rushes to her own open slider door and sees the woman across the room, opening a carved front door.

"Stop right there. Stop." Beth yells, running towards the woman, who goes outside and closes the door after herself. At that moment, Beth finds herself standing in front of her own front door. The door the woman went through is gone.

Stunned by what she's seen, Beth opens her own door and looks outside. At that moment, she hears a crash and turns to see that Maxine has knocked the pitcher of water off the bedside stand and has slipped halfway off the hospital bed. Racing to her, Beth lifts her back onto the bed. Moaning loudly, Maxine asks, "Beth, Beth, no more, please, no more. Beth? Where...?"

Sobbing, Beth holds Maxine in her arms and cries, "I'm here, Max. I'm here, my darling."

Maxine breathes out one last time, "Beth, wonderful, wonder..."

THREE

June 1—Eliza

ELIZA takes the stairs up to the third floor of her beautifully redone cabin/home at Redcliff's Beach. At the top of the landing, she looks across the open space and is glad the room was added to the original plan. As she looks around the open room, she understands why her sister, Marie, decided to call the space 'the W's', short for 'widow's walk'. The term comes from the rooms built at the top of Victorian homes for wives of sea captains to watch for loved ones returning from months at sea. When Marie suggested the idea, Eliza quickly agreed and, on this first morning in her new home, she is pleased to see what a charming addition it makes to their ocean front home. The room has the comfort of a den with sofas and chairs facing a propane fireplace along the north wall. Out the row of glass doors facing the beach, Eliza sees a spacious lanai with several high backed wicker chairs.

Last year, Eliza told Marie she would like to live full time at Redcliff's Beach. She asked her sister, if she could rebuild their father's original cabin into a fully functional home. An established architect/designer, Marie jumped at the chance and told Eliza she would design and oversee the rebuild. This morning, Eliza loves everything she sees in the space and is very grateful Marie took on their project. It was Marie who decided to reuse the original kitchen, from their Dad's cabin, on this floor. Now, Eliza understands why her sister was so insistent.

Walking over to the old familiar cabinets, she runs her fingers over the countertop as she looks out the venting windows along the east wall. Marie added the powder room at the top of the staircase, insisting it was for her own comforts. It was also Marie who decided not change the footprint of the original cabin, but to build up two full stories for the space they wanted.

This first morning in their new home, Eliza is pleased with all that she sees and especially how smoothly the past week's move was completed. Stopping next to the kitchen counter, she fills the espresso machine with water and coffee beans and pushes the buttons to make her favorite hot brew. The delicious aroma fills the room and when the machine finishes, Eliza fills a mug, adds a shot of whipped cream and takes the drink out to the lanai.

Sinking into the pillows on the nearest wicker chair, she sips and watches Redcliff's Beach wake up. Stars still wink on and off in predawn grey of the western horizon as the sun hasn't yet broken over the Coastal Mountains Range to the east. The lanai sits so far off the beach few sounds reach her except for the scream of a gull or two which soar past to settle down at the edge of the incoming waves.

One bold grey-gull lands gently onto the railing closest to her chair and eyes the area for stray goodies. Laughing, Eliza shoos it away with a clap of her hands, as she knows seagulls learn quickly about who feeds them and who doesn't.

Along the waves, pre-dawn joggers head north to the red cliffs, which give Redcliff's Beach its name and Eliza remembers how she raced Marie to be the first one to slap their touchstone in the cliff face. Now that the house is finished, she worries how Marie is going to adjust to her life without her husband, Jim Hall. The dear man died of a heart attack a week after Eliza suggested redoing the cabin, yet, when she suggested getting another architect for the rebuild, Marie was adamant that she needed the project to remind her that she could still live.

Before a single board was removed, Marie, insisted each be marked and carefully stored for later reuse. The grandest use of material is the cabin's copper roofing which was lifted in total off the framework and, when the expanded restructured framing was ready, it was carefully replaced onto the rebuild. In fact, Marie reused most of the materials from the original cabin and, everywhere Eliza looks, she sees materials which bring back memories and add charm to the home.

To top it off, Marie finished the remodel a month early as she knew Eliza planned to retire and move to the beach. This month gave them time to setup their suites, on the second floor, and to decorate the main floor common room which was the original cabin's total space. All interior walls were removed and the entry expanded next to the new staircase to the upper floors. The stone fireplace was scrubbed, re-grouted in a few places and now shines as if brand new.

Wide decks replaced old ones and a north side deck was added to flow around the stonework of the fireplace. The new beach deck was extended twenty feet to the west and became the roof for a pair of twin suites for Marie's daughters to use whenever they visit.

Sipping her coffee, Eliza mentally checks off the highs and lows of the last couple of months, 'When I told Jack I was leaving to live at Redcliff's Beach, he thought I meant to Dad's old cabin. I never explained what Marie was doing as it had nothing to do with him. Fortunately, my lawyer insisted I finalize the divorce before I put money towards the house. I told Jack only that I would be living at the cabin and, I guess in a many ways I am.

'At least the cabin floor is the same as Dad put in his cabin and Marie used most of the materials in our new home. The new kitchen is wonderful and I can't believe how beautiful Dad's concrete floor looks with the dark stain we chose. It really highlights that hunk of glowing agate Dad put under the dining table.'

Closing her eyes, Eliza lets the sounds of incoming waves take her back to yesterday's retirement party from being CEO at Staples' Fruit Packing Company for the past twenty years. She'd said goodbye to all and enjoyed every minute. Smiling, she lets her memories of the day flow past. 'Jack actually seemed to step into his new position with some *grace. I gave him the chance to show his stuff as his replacing me was Mina's only dying wish and I could never deny my darling mother in law anything. Mina turned her stock in the company and the mansion over to me as she realized, years before, that the Board would never tolerate Jack's drinking and womanizing. However, yesterday he kept to a minimum and was polite to everyone. It surprised all of us, especially me.*

'By the time his father, Mel Staples, died, Jack's hard reputation had shocked Mina, so she put me up for the position and backed her decision by giving me all her voting stock. When he heard, Jack threatened to kill us both. Mina got an injunction against his coming close to the Mansion or either of us. He left town for a couple years and only came back when he heard Mina was dying. She told him then, that when I retired, he would have a chance to prove himself if he worked hard until that time. Now he has it and time will tell how he does with the opportunity.

Running her fingers through her thick shoulder length white hair, Eliza laughs, "Good riddance to both Staples Fruit Packing Company and the Jack-ass who now runs it. I gave many good years to each. Jack couldn't believe it when I finally divorced him and was doubly dumbfounded when I announced my intention to retire. It was at that time that I told him I would uphold Mina's wish for him to replace me and he could live at the Mansion as long as I lived. After that, it goes to the School District. Hell, we spoke hardly ten words after Mina died and I was more alone at Staples Mansion than I will ever be here at Redcliff's Beach.

Taking the stairs down to the second floor landing, Eliza goes into her suite and straight into bathroom. Hanging her robe on a hook on the back of the bathroom door, she stands in front of the mirrored wall and turns from side to side, scrutinizing her naked body. Slapping both cheeks of her ample bottom, she shakes her head, "That ass is too big and it time for it to go. Running to the cliffs to slap my touchstone starts this week, as soon as I'm settled."

Stepping into the spa-sized shower, she turns on the sprays and sees the round gold tile set into middle of the blue tiled wall. Smiling, Eliza slaps the golden tile and shouts, "I declare this run is good and done."

Then, she feels the need to wash off whatever angst is left from years of living with Jack and scrubs her body twice, everywhere. Finally, she rinses in the spray until she feels totally cleansed and ready to live life on her own terms.

Dressing quickly, in shorts and a loose silk shirt, she heads down to the new modern kitchen and opens the fridge for something to fix for breakfast. Seeing only jars and bottles of condiments, she remembers Marie told her to shop for groceries on the way out to the house. "Well that settles it, today I shop. Filling cupboards and pantry has to come first, so running the beach will just have to wait a day or two."

Grabbing her purse, she goes into the garage and sees the new blue BMW she'd given herself as a retirement gift. Next to it sits the old Jeep Mina bought years ago, to use at the beach. Mina had named it Charlie. Eliza smiles at the memory of when she'd asked her mother-in-law to come to the cabin with her. The darling older woman had yelled "Wahoo, I'll say I do."

On the way to the beach, they'd passed a used car lot which had an old Army 'Jeep' place on a platform with flags and balloons tied all over it. Mina had insisted they turn around and go look at it. For Mina had been love at first sight, she wrote a check for the full price, named the Jeep 'Charlie' and drove it to the cabin with Eliza, in her car, leading the way. After that, whenever the two women came to the beach, they drove 'Charlie' to town or on the beach. Mina took great joy in telling her friends and husband, Mel, about the wild rides Charlie gave them, omitting that Charlie was a Jeep. Not even her husband, Mel, knew for many years and Mina loved Eliza even more for keeping her secret.

"Charlie, you're still the main man here at the beach. No sense exposing that beautiful new Beemer to any more salt air than necessary." Tossing her purse on the Jeep's passenger seat, Eliza turns the key in the starter and the engine kicks over on the first try. Smiling, Eliza says, "Charlie, we may both be showing our years, but it looks as if we both have some kick still in us and I'll expect to have the same wild rides you gave Mina."

Backing out the garage, onto the cobblestoned driveway, she waits until the garage door shuts tight. Looking across the front of her home, Eliza is pleased by what she sees, "It's still the cabin but now so much more. That widow's walk sits high above neighboring roofs and I love how the wide eaves cover the new decks. It's great that Marie kept the elaborate arbor. No one should ever doubt where to find the front door."

Turning the Jeep within the circular driveway, Eliza pulls up to Shoreline Drive and heads south. As she passes her mailbox, she sees her neighbors, Al and Penny Goodwin, standing next to their own, at the top of their own driveway. Slowing to a stop, Eliza rolls down the Jeep's window and, before she can speak, Al shouts through to her. "Hello Eliza. We saw you come in last night. Good to have you back at the beach. The tides are great this week. The afternoon's low is a minus eight at two thirty. Will we see you out there?"

"Thanks for the info, Al. It's good to see you both, too. No beach for me today though, I've a larder to fill and unpacking to be done, too much for any beach time, I'm afraid. By the way, thanks for getting Charlie in for his lube job last week. I owe you a big bottle of your favorite."

"Enjoyed driving him, Eliza, he's a great little buggy." Al laughs.

At that, Penny pushes past Al and pokes her head into the window, and asks, "Jack won't be coming here anymore, will he? Didn't the divorce become final last month?" When she sees Eliza's surprised look, the woman continues, "You know how the beach crowd loves you and Mina and Marie and her twins, but we dreaded the times Jack turned up. You have to admit, that man ruined any party he went to, making lewd comments and hitting on all the women on the beach. Which reminds me, I'm having the gang over for dinner tomorrow night. Could you make it?"

"Wonderful, I'd love to come. I'll bring pie and ice cream as I know that's Al's favorite dessert." Eliza laughs and waves goodbye, "See you then."

The many changes along Shoreline Drive surprise Eliza, as it had been dark when she'd driven in last night. As soon as she rounds the south curve and zips up the hill, she is met with a stretch of stone walls covered with flags and signs indicating a development of new homes amongst wind-twisted shore pines along the south cliffs at that end of Redcliff's Beach. Continuing down Shoreline Drive, she sees that the Sand Dollar Casino has added a long wing to its hotel.

When the road drops back along the beach, she sees vehicles racing down the hard packed sand and says, "Look at that, Charlie, the tide isn't even out and the beach is going crazy. Maybe we'll go out after we get the groceries home and stored. We could both use a good run to blow the carbon out of our systems. Besides, it's time I shed these pounds so I can race Marie to the north cliffs. I want to shout, 'I declare this run is good and done.'

Eliza sighs, "It's lucky that Dad got our end of the beach turned into the State Park. Busy as it gets, it's got the wildness that was there when Marie and I were kids. Those high red cliffs holds our touchstone and if it weren't part of the park, someone would have dug that melon-sized agate out of the cliff face by now."

Sudden emotions boil up within Eliza and she begins to cry. Pulling to the side of the road, she grabs tissue from the box under the dash and wipes her eyes. "What the hell is this about? I guess there is too much coming at me. Whew, Charlie, I feel weak. Why am I shaking so much? The move didn't overwhelm me. I love being here. Probably need some breakfast, it's nearly ten. I'll put a good meal into both of us, Charlie. I see your gas gage says you're nearly on empty."

Pulling back on Shoreline Drive, Eliza feels lightheaded and drives slowly to the Y cutoff. When cars behind honk, she waves them around and turns on her flashers to caution other drivers. Turning off the road into Ocean Shores, she drives into the gas station and pulls up to one of the gas pumps. While the young attendant fills the tank, Eliza thinks over her years with Jack. "Why did I stay with that asshole for so long? When Mina turned Staple Fruit Packing Company over to me, I stopped worrying about not having children. I loved the work and nothing else mattered. I was busy and happy. Funny how things happen, a month ago, I was dining with an old doctor friend and our discussion turned to families, When I mentioned how hard I had tried to get pregnant, he was shocked and told me he had cut Jack's tubes because he'd said I'd didn't want a family. Charlie, I was heartbroken. Thank God, Mina never knew this blackest mark on her son's soul. It would have killed her."

Closing her eyes, Eliza's mind whirls. *That bastard, Mel Staples, should have been shot for the way he treated Mina. Luckily, he died before Mina and she inherited the Staples Mansion and the voting stock which she passed to me. Jack went crazy and threatened to kill me. Mina took me to her lawyers to rewrite my will and get it filed. After that, Jack was paid two hundred thousand a year, whether he worked or not. He gets to live in the Mansion as long as I live.*

How surprised he was when I divorced him and told him I was retiring and moving out here to the beach. I had to remind him, again, that he lives at the Mansion only as long as I live.

A tapping on the window startles Eliza back to the present and she hands her credit card to the attendant. When he returns with the slip, she signs it and at that time sees how hard her hands are shaking. "What is this? Low blood sugar? Where's that drive-in?" Looking over her shoulder, she sees it is attached to the far side of the service station and starts the Jeep. However, before she can drive to it, a large red pickup stops next to the Jeep and a man calls to her, "How's the house fitting you, Mrs. Staples?" Recognizing Stan Morris, the developer who'd worked with Marie to build their house, Eliza answers, "It's wonderful, Stan, and, please, call me Eliza. Stop by and see the good work your company did with Marie's design and guidance."

After he drives away, Eliza turns the Jeep up to the drive-up window and orders a large cheeseburger with all the trimmings. When the food arrives, she parks the Jeep and bolts down the food, then waits for the shaking and nausea to ease. Finally admitting her sickness is worsening, Eliza clutches the steering wheel and cries, "Charlie, why do I feel so bad? I should be happy. I'm at the beach. I love the beach. Why is my body out of control? I haven't felt this way for years. Not since I was diagnosed as bipolar manic depressive and got meds that balanced me out. I take them twice a day, every day. Oh no, Charlie? My meds, Charlie, I didn't take my meds this morning. How could I forget? I always take them right before I shower. Didn't I? No, I didn't and I didn't take them last night. Oh Charlie, I've missed two full doses.

"Oh, dear God, my meds. If I didn't take them when I got to the cabin, where are they? I took them yesterday, before my retirement party. I must have left the medicine next to the sink... at the Mansion. Right where I was sure to see it and bring it with me. But I didn't, Charlie. I went out the front door and I've missed two full doses. Charlie, we've got to go get them. Right now, Charlie, we've got to go back right now and get my meds."

Without any more thought, Eliza turns the Jeep onto the road that goes from the beach, across the Coastal Mountain Range, over the freeways and stops at Staples' Mansion. As she speeds through small towns along the way, she does so without really seeing anything. In two hours, she turns onto the I-5 Freeway heading south and follows the signs to the bridge over the Columbia River. On the other side of the river, she passes three exits into Portland until she sees the exit onto I-80 East and follows it.

Her mind spins in all directions, "Jack Staples loved me at first. I wouldn't have settled for less. For ten years, before that damned Mel decided I should know how to handle guns, so I could hunt with Jack. I loaded, shot, cleaned, each of Mel's damned gun collection, over and over. Yeah, Jack loved me then. Then Mel turned him into the same bastard as he was. That broke Mina's heart. Tore my heart out and ended everything I felt for him. Lucky for Mina, Mel died of a heart attack or she would have killed him. Of course, I never mentioned to anyone how his liqueur got laced with a couple of Castor Beans cooked up just for him."

Pushing the Jeep to its maximum speed, Eliza watches the exit numbers flash past until Charlie turns, off I-80, onto the exit they need. After they cross the overpass, they turn up the hill then stop at the iron gates which block the road. Eliza automatically punches numbers into the keypad and waits till the gates open. Then, Charlie drives on up the hill, turns into a lane that rounds a grove of evergreens and stops at the rear of the large Victorian Mansion. For several seconds, Eliza sits trying to remember why she's there. Finally, she stumbles up to the back door and goes inside. Again she automatically keys in numbers to shut off the alarm and runs to the kitchen.

Her medicine bag sits on the counter, next to the sink and she unzips it. Dumping the bottles onto the counter, she counts out the required pills for the two does. Filling a tall glass with water, she swallows both sets of meds, then sighs with relief. By this time, Eliza is shaking so hard the water sloshes out of the glass and she leans on the counter for several minutes. She only thinks of how close she came to losing herself for several months.

Looking at the clock on the micro-wave, she shudders, "My God it's nearly noon. Too close for comfort and too stupid for words. Now I'll need to sleep at least till three, maybe four, before I drive back to the beach. No hurry though. I'll get back in time to shop and get the dessert for Penny and Al's dinner party tomorrow night."

Slowly, her nausea settles and Eliza scoops the medicine bottles back into the medicine bag and takes it out to the Jeep. Tucking it under the passenger seat next to her purse, she also slips the Jeep's key into the ignition, then goes back in the house to sleep a few hours.

When back in the kitchen, Eliza slaps together a peanut butter and jelly sandwich and drinks a large glass of water with it. After rinsing the glass and knife, she puts them into the dishwasher then wipes off the counter and her face with a wet paper towel and tosses it into the garbage under the sink.

Yawning widely, she walks through the house to the wide circular foyer and looks out the sidelight of the carved entry doors. Turning to go up the sweeping staircase to the upper floors and her old bedroom, she changes her mind and, instead, walks to the set of French doors to the right of the staircase. Opening one of the doors, Eliza steps into a large room which Mina had called the Library. The room stretches the full width along the rear of the Staples Mansion where a wide flagstone veranda is surrounded by "seating high" stonewalls that overlook the Columbia River Gorge far below.

The room is paneled with mahogany and has several glass enclosed cabinets which show off Grandfather Staples' collections of first editions, awards, artifacts, antique pistols and rifles. The leather furniture is old and massive and the floors are teak decking from an old sailing ship that sank off Portland's first harbor. Here and there, the dark floor is splashed with colorful Turkish rugs. Above, the ceiling is paneled with bleached oak and a massive native stone fireplace covers the end wall where the sofas and chairs are gathered for conversation and comfort.

Eliza walks over to stand in front of the glass cases holding Grandfather Staples collection of antique pistols, rifles, holsters, with boxes of ammunition for each gun beside it. These are the guns Eliza shot and cleaned when she still loved Jack. Staring at the last gun she'd handled, she hisses. "There you are, you rarest of antiques. I dropped you on purpose that last time and Mel knew it. That's why he cussed me up one side and down the other. I shouted at him to go burn in hell and that I was no longer his whipping post." At the thought of Mel Staples amongst hot flames, Eliza laughs loudly, too loudly and too long.

"No wonder I avoided this room after Mina's death. There is nothing for me in here." A wide sucking yawn tells her the pills are taking effect and Eliza pulls two old throws off the ends of the leather sofas, lays one over the cushions on one sofa and tucks a small pillow at one end. Then, she lays down and pulls the second throw over her legs. As soon as her head touches the pillow, she is asleep.

A blast of sound startles Eliza awake and she stumbles to her feet with her heart pounding wildly in her ears. Looking around the room, she tries to remember where she is. Seeing nothing that could have caused such a noise, she is puzzled and her headache pounds in her ears, so much so, that she drops onto the sofa holding her head in her hands, moaning softly. It is some while before she opens her eyes and tries to focus them. Seeing the stone fireplace, Eliza at first thinks she is in her own home until more of the room comes into focus and realizes she's at the Mansion though it takes several seconds for her to remember why she is here. Her watch says it close to two. "Damn, I need more sleep before I can drive to the beach."

Standing slowly, she moves to the open French door and looks into the foyer, sees the doors are shut, so she shouts, "Hello? Anybody there?" As if an answer, a horn blasts from outside and Eliza jumps back into the room. Then a woman's screech of laughter and a man's voice yelling, "I'm so horny I'm honking," tells Eliza what is happening.

A harsh rush of old emotions crash through Eliza and vomit fills her mouth. Rushing into the kitchen, she spits the bitter liquid into the sink and shakes with anger, rage surging through her. These same emotions she'd felt too often, every time Jack had openly strutted his latest slut through their small community, a dozen or more by her count. Walking back to the entry doors, she looks out the side light and sees Jack's Mercedes is parked at the front steps and rocking wildly. Two people can be seen grappling on the front seat through the front window of the car. As she watches, clothes are tossed out of the driver's window and land on the wide front stoop.

Spinning away, Eliza races through the kitchen to the maid's bathroom, collapses beside the toilet bowl and vomits. Residue of medications and sandwich swirl in the toilet water. Shaking uncontrollably, she spits the foulness into it until the dry heaves stop.

When the spasms cease, Eliza wipes her mouth with a wad of toilet paper and flushes it down. Leaning against the washbasin, she splashes cold water over her face and rinses her mouth until the bitter taste is gone. Drying with a hand towel, she wipes the sink and toilet, then drops the towel in the laundry hamper with other dirty laundry.

Finally, she shuts the lid of the toilet and sits with her head in her hands trying to think of what to do. "Why do I care so much? What more do I have to take? What else can he do to me? Thank God, we never had children, neither for Mina, nor for me. What a horrid father he'd have been. I spent years with that bastard fucking every woman around. He has to be stopped. I will no longer be the butt of dirty jokes or hear snickers as I pass. That bastard will never shame me again! Never again!"

In that instant, she knows what she must do. Hurrying into the kitchen, she opens the cabinet under the sink and takes a pair of rubber gloves from an open box, tosses the box back in the cabinet and slams the door closed. As she walks back to the library, she pulls the gloves on her hands and goes directly to the glassed cabinet holding the gun of her choice, Grandfather Staples' old pistol, the one she'd dropped years ago.

Reaching down the right side of the cabinet's molding, she feels the button and presses it. Hearing the click of the lock, Eliza steps aside and lets the glass doors swing open. Reaching inside, she lifts the heavy pistol off its sterling silver display rack, as well as, the box of ammunition next to it. "Grandfather Staples, your old-west six-shooter is going to kill me a dirty rotten rat." Eliza's smile twists as she speaks, "After the rabid dogs you killed with this gun, my doing in one more rotten bastard won't matter one damned bit to anyone."

As if it were yesterday, Eliza remembers what Mel Staples had drilled into her head and opens the gun's barrel, takes six bullets from the ammo box and slips one into each of the six chambers. Then she snaps the gun shut in one quick motion. Walking to a wing-backed chair, she turns it to face the open French door and sits.

Almost instantly, as if timed to her sitting in the chair, one entry door bangs open and Eliza raises the gun and points it at the entry. When nothing further happens, she lowers the pistol back to her lap and waits. Then, in a swirl of movement, two naked people rush inside and stop at the bottom step of the sweeping three story staircase. Eliza walks to the door and sees Jack Staples, her ex-husband, grasping the buttocks of a woman he's lifted to carry. For several seconds, he grinds his pelvis into hers, then they move slowly up the stairs, one step at a time. Disgusted, Eliza turns to look at the open doorway and stares the clothes scattered on the stoop. A small suitcase sits on the threshold of the doorway.

Though the naked couple can no longer be seen, a rush of hate rages through Eliza and she shakes so hard she is unable to move. When shrieks of laughter, shouted obscenities and orgasmic bellows rain down from upstairs, Eliza runs back to the chair and plugs her ears trying to block the obscene sounds.

After several minutes, there is only silence. Then, running water can be heard from somewhere above. Suddenly, as if a naked puppet,

Jack appears leaping down the stairs and yelling, "Get your ass in that tub woman! I'll get the drinks."

A woman yells, "Forget the damn wine, Jack. Get that big cock back in here. I need it now."

More laughter erupts from both people, on separate floors, that echoes through the house. Eliza raises the gun off her lap and points it at the open French door. However, Jack races past the room without seeing her. Soon loud banging of cabinet doors and slamming of drawers comes from the kitchen. A minute later, the naked man races back past the open door holding a large bottle of wine and two fluted glasses high over his head, shouting, "Ready or not here I come!"

Only then does Eliza go to the open French door and watches Jack bounce up the stairs. Numb, Eliza moves without feeling her legs or body as she walks to the open entry door. Frowning with disgust, she pokes at the discarded clothing and small suitcase with the toe of her shoe. Then, she follows Jack up the stairs to the first landing wondering what she will say to him as she shoots his slut.

The thought brings a bubble of laughter into her throat that's caught and held there. At the landing, she turns left and goes down the hall to the door to Jack's suite of rooms. Silently, she turns the knob and opens the door and goes through his sitting room and throws open his bedroom door. When the door hits the wall with a slam, Eliza is pointing the gun, ready to shoot and is stopped by a neatly made bed.

There is no one inside the room. No one is lying across Jack's bed. Stunned, she tries to think where they could be, then a shriek comes from the opposite end of the long hall. The sound hits Eliza as if a blow to her midsection and her breath leaves in a rush. Her heart pounds inside her chest and her head throbs with an unbearable hatred for the man. Hissing the words, Eliza growls, "That bastard. He's taken his slut to my bedroom. He's rutting on my bed."

Rage propels her down the hall and through the open door to the suite of rooms which had been hers for thirty years and Eliza hears Jack groan and a woman giggle. As she enters the room, Jack's groans come faster and Eliza moves to the foot of the large bed. In the middle of a heap of bedding, she sees what looks to be a strangely shaped being. In the next instant, she realizes it is a woman's buttocks and the woman's head buried into Jack's crotch.

When Jack thrusts his groin at the woman's face and his hands pull at her thick black hair, Eliza aims the gun and pulls the trigger, shooting the woman directly through the back of her head into Jack's groin. Instantly, Jack's head pops up and he looks wild eyed at Eliza. Instantly, she shoots him, twice more, once in his chest and once in his forehead, contract killer style, clean and neat.

For several seconds, Eliza stares at the bodies, watching for signs of life. When there is no further movement, she tips the gun upward and blows the smoke from the barrel end. "The only good rat is a dead rat." It is then that the bubble of laughter caught in her throat bursts out as a sob and she takes the actions needed as if following a checklist.

Turn air conditioner to forty degrees to keep bodies cold to make time of death hard to determine. No fingerprints left as used rubber gloves. Shut bedroom door. Shut suite door. Go back to library. Clean gun and ammo. Return all to cabinet. Make library as found. Leave by back door. Toss gloves into river.

When Eliza reaches the open entry downstairs, she stares at Jack's car parked close to the front stoop, the driver's door open. For a few seconds, she considers moving it to the garage and shutting the entry doors. Then, the sight of scattered clothes and the suitcase on the threshold stops her.

Going back to the library, she lays the pistol on the rumpled throws on the sofa, walks to the open cabinet, presses a faded mark on the bottom and, when trap door opens, she lifts the gun-cleaning kit from its hidden location. Eliza smiles as she recognizes the one she'd used years before.

Carrying the kit to the sofa, she pulls the pistol apart and cleans it thoroughly. Then she wipes each empty shell-casing and unused bullets before she returns them to the ammo box. Reassembling the pistol, she wipes off each part and does the same to the box of ammo. Then she carefully refolds the cleaning rag, puts it back into the kit and places the kit back into its place in the gun cabinet. Lastly, she places the cleaned pistol on its silver display rack and sets the ammo box exactly where it had sat. Then, she pushes the glass doors of the cabinet closed until she hears the firm click of the lock.

Walking to the sofa, where she'd napped, she folds the two throws and lays them exactly where they'd been on the backs of the leather sofas. After patting the small pillow back into its original spot, Eliza turns the wing-backed chair back to face the fireplace and scans the large room for any other sign she'd been there. When she is sure there is nothing out of place, Eliza peels each rubber glove off her hands and tucks one inside the other to form a small tight ball. Then, with a great sense of relief, and no sense of loss or guilt, Eliza goes out the French door, kicking it closed with her foot.

Carrying the ball of rubber gloves in her left hand, she walks through the kitchen and out the back door, leaving it open behind her. As she slips onto the driver's seat of the Jeep, Eliza pats the steering wheel and says, "Okay, Charlie, let's go home, we've had a long day."

At the gate entrance, Eliza is keying the numbers to open it, when it begins to rain. "Rain is good, Charlie. It'll wash away your tire marks and no one will ever know we were here." Continuing to talk to the Jeep as if it were her friend, they drive west on I-80 and Eliza tells Charlie everything that happened inside Staple's Mansion. She finishes her story by saying she feels the pleasure of a job well done. When they are halfway across the Columbia River Bridge, the rain turns into a downpour and traffic slows to a crawl. At that time, Eliza pulls into the far right lane, opens the Jeep's window, sticks out her left arm and heaves the balled gloves up over the top of the Jeep, and the bridge railing, into the river far below.

FOUR

June 5—Liz

LIZ loses the week following Peter's death. Nothing seems to matter to her anymore as the one person she valued above her own life is gone. Peter's death leaves a void into which she's fallen and can't seem to find her way out. Though she manages to move through each day, greeting and thanking family and visitors, she does so without feeling or notice. Alexandria comes daily with offers to help sort through Peter's things. Each day, Liz sends her neighbor away with a shake of her head and a wave of her hand. Liz finds her only solace at the edge of the waves, before dawn or late at night, trekking north to the red cliffs and her touchstone where she talks to Peter as she did her family.

On the morning of the fifth of June, Peter's ashes arrive by Federal Express. Taking the package from the FedEx driver, Liz is forced to face this harsh reality of life. Holding the neatly wrapped package in both hands, she is shocked that the compact package could hold the remains of Peter. Carrying the package to the kitchen counter, she slits the wrapping with a small knife and pulls out a sturdy black box. Peter's full name is typed on a large label laid carefully across the top with the words, "CREMATION NUMBER 2200991" directly under is his name.

Lifting off the lid of the box, she sees a clear plastic bag filled with ash. Taking the bag from the box, Liz studies the contents through the clear plastic, trying to get her mind around what the next step should be.

Looking out the north window at the waves, she sees the tide has changed and the exposed tide flats are attracting both shorebirds and clam-diggers. This fact makes her decision easy. Slitting the bag of ashes with a knife, she put it into a small daypack, shrugs it over her shoulders and heads onto the beach.

Keeping her focus on the north red cliffs, Liz follows the edge of the outgoing waves and talks to Peter, "We always said we'd spread each other's ash on the first ebbing tide, Peter, and this is the first ebbing tide today. I'd keep you on the mantle forever, my darling, but you said if I did that you'd haunt me until I did what you wanted. Therefore, my love, I'm taking you to the red cliffs and will lay you on this outgoing tide."

As she reaches the base of the cliffs, Liz walks along the edge of the smooth granite slab, swings the pack off her shoulders and sets it the huge red boulder. The few people near the cliffs are too absorbed in their adventures to give her more than a brief glance. When she lifts the bag of ash from the pack, a rush of strong emotion nearly overwhelms her and she presses the bag to her chest for several minutes.

When her feeling of loss softens, Liz walks across the tide flats, passing tide pools filled with shells, anemones, snails and starfish, until she reaches the waves. Holding the bag of ash tightly to her, she wades into the waves until she can feel the pull of the undertow on her legs. At that time, she holds the bag of ash out from her, tips the slit end to one side and lets the ash pour slowly onto the outgoing waves.

"Go with God my love, you are done with this life. Be free and soar through the Universe. I love you. I always will. I release your ashes upon these waters, at this place you have loved for so many years, Redcliff's Beach."

The ash swirls away as it mixes with the waves and disappears. Shaking the bag, the last bit of dust is grabbed by the breeze and carried up to the cliff tops and Liz stares after it long after there is nothing to see. Wadding back to the granite slab, she stuffs the plastic bag into the backpack, slings one strap over a shoulder and steps onto the granite slab. Going directly across to the translucent touchstone in the cliff face, Liz puts her hand upon the stone and whispers, "I declare Peter Day's life is good and done!"

Tears don't come until Liz is back home, curled up in Peter's chair with his old woolen throw wrapped around her. Then she cries herself to sleep. When she awakens, hours later, the house is dark and she turns on the reading lamp next to the chair. Her watch shows it's nearly midnight and Liz hears rain hitting the north windows. Going to the slider door, Liz opens it to look out at the beach and smell the rain. When she closes the slider door, she sees a bright light reflected on the window. Staring at the reflection, she can tell it doesn't come from the reading lamp near the chair, but is right behind her, from over the dining table.

Turning, she sees the agate in the floor, under the table, is glowing brighter. However, the brightest light is coming from the ceiling. Stunned, Liz watches the lights pulse at the same beat as if sharing information. First the one from the ceiling brightens, then the agate within the floor does the same. Then, both dim and brighten as if pulsing in time with some unheard tune.

Liz has loved the soft glow, from the agate in the floor, ever since she was a child. However, there has never been a light over the dining table and she knows there is no wiring in the ceiling nor in the floor above. There has never been, nor should there be, light coming from that location in the ceiling. Walking past the dining table, she goes to sit in the chair where she'd slept and, from there, she sees the glow from the agate in the floor has intensified in response to the bright light from above.

Puzzled, she walks around the table several times, looking at the ceiling and at the floor. Several times, she puts her hand into the beam of light beam to see if she can feel what it is. When her hand casts a shadow onto the table, Liz whispers, "There's no way light should come through the ceiling. This is crazy making, absolutely impossible."

Getting onto her knees, she studies the agate in the floor. She and

Dana played under the table for years, using the stone as their playhouse table on rainy days. Never, during all those years, had the stone ever shone as brightly as it does at this moment.

Touching the stone's surface, the light intensifies and pulses rapidly as if in anger and Liz backs away from it, shouting, "What the hell has happened to this rock brought home fifty years ago? It's brighter now than when sunlight hits it and it's the middle of the night." Walking to the lamp, she turns it off and sees that the lights from above and below the table keep the room well lit.

Liz sees the light from above now covers the entire surface of the table and there are three shadows moving within it. Sudden chills cover her arms and Liz flicks on the gas fireplace. Sitting on edge of the sofa, she watches the flames for several minutes trying to ignore the fact that the shadows in the beam of light are becoming recognizable people. In the corner of her eye, Liz sees a tall blond young man holding his hands out to her.

Gasping, Liz turns to stares at the image and cries out, "Peter, go away, you can't come back. You died. You're gone. Go away. Please. Go away." Sobbing, Liz rushes at the table and pounds on it. Instantly, the beam of light, with the Peter's image, vanishes and the room darkens. The stone in the floor glows softly as it always had for years. Shaking, Liz returns to the sofa and tries to decide what she should do next.

Her answer comes in the next minute when the light beam returns and covers the surface of the dining table. In it is the image of Peter as a young man and behind him are two other people facing rooms which seems attached to hers yet within another space. Liz screams at the vision, "Damn it, Peter, I told you to go away. I don't want to see you. You're not real. Don't come back." Again, Liz rushes at the table and as her hands smack its surface, the vision disappears.

However, the moment she turns away, the light returns and Liz begins to cry. "Peter, why are you doing this to me? I put you onto the outgoing tide this morning. You are part of the Universe. Please, go away. I never knew you when you were as you look... oh, okay, well, now you look as you did when we first met at the University. You were twenty five and I was twenty. Good grief, were we ever that young? Those other people with you, who are they? I don't know them."

Though Peter's image doesn't answer, the other two become clearer and Liz sees that the person to his right is a beautiful dark woman talking to someone standing by a slider door. However, the person to Peter's left is a handsome man with flame red hair who shakes his fists at a woman on a sofa near the fireplace. Liz has to look twice to see she is not on Liz's own sofa.

While Liz watches the images, the clothing on all three changes, from the modern street clothes they'd been wearing, to long flowing white robes which shimmer as the people move.

At that time, Liz sees the others within the light beam face two women much the same as she is and whose houses are the same as hers. Though she can see the rooms are not in the same place hers is, Liz can tell they are linked to her home. As Liz studies the women in their homes, neither seems to see her or her home or react to the person, in the light, who watches them.

After several minutes, Liz hears a familiar voice speaking softly inside her head. Knowing it is Peter's voice, she turns to look at his image and sees his lips move with each word. At first, she does not understand what he says, but she feels his words flow through her. Then, as if adjusting to her need, Peter's voice clears and it is as if he were seated next to her on the sofa. From that moment, Peter's image becomes solid within the light beam and his voice fills her mind.

He speaks slowly at first, then he speaks faster and faster until Liz is pulled through every second, of every minute, of every day, of every week, of every month, of every year of their life together. Visions flip though her mind with such intense speed, they blur. When the frames reach to the present, the visions slow, then halt at the moment she waved him off on his last flight. At first, Liz's mind reels from the furious speed and feels so dizzy she closes her eyes. For over an hour, she lays on the sofa in a deep sleep.

When Liz finally opens her eyes, she knows the terrible void, felt since Peter's death, is gone. She feels as if born anew and knows her true self has returned. There is no sense of sorrow nor of loss. Instead, she feels joyous energy for life and again looks to the future. Seeing Peter's image within the light beam on the dining table, his words embrace her in soft rhythms. Each word coming to her as if a loving caress.

Elizabeth Ann live as you wish, not as others want. Love all ways and love always. Let no one turn you from your true path through life. Be grateful for what you are given and be thankful for what you have to give. Embrace whoever or whatever brings you joy. Embrace the being you are. Know you exist all ways, in all ways, at all times. Choose each experience wisely and learn from that which you chose. Each is your teacher. Learn the lessons brought to you. Know other ways may not be your way. Grow within each life experience. Greet each lesson given whether negative or positive and apply that lesson to your future. Avoid negative beings as their life paths must be repeated until that life's lesson is learned and embraced. Fear no one. Trust and honor yourself through your actions. Know there are no mistakes. Know wisdom and joy are yours for you are a goddess. Love all ways and love always.

Then beam deepens to amber gold and Peter's voice becomes harsh. Frightened, Liz cringes from the vision and yells, "Stop that, Peter. Don't speak to me like that. I can't understand what you want me to do. What? Why should I call Alex? Why? Tell her to come over here?" Though puzzled by his harshness, Liz picks up her cellphone and calls Alex. When her neighbor answers, Liz shouts, "Alex? Liz. Come over right now. Peter has come back and wants to talk to you. Yes, he's come back. He's been telling me many things and he says it's time to speak to you. Yes, Alex, Peter's here within a beam of light. Yes, he is and he wants to see you right now. Come over and see him for yourself." Then, without waiting for Alex's response, Liz hangs up, "Okay, Peter, I've called Alex. What else do you want?"

Nothing happens for the next half hour, then footsteps can be heard running along the north side deck and stopping at the slider door. Surprised to see Alexandria Petrow peering through the glass door, Liz yells, "Alex, come in and sit by me on the sofa. Alex? Don't you see where I am?"

Slowly walking through the slider door, Alex stares at Liz. "Liz? You okay? You said Peter has come back here? Liz? Your Peter died, Liz. He's dead. Peter could not be here. How am I going to talk with him? I don't see him anywhere in here."

"Oh, Alex, come here and sit beside me. Here on the sofa, that's right. Sit right there and be quiet. Good. Now look over at the top of the dining table. Do you see the beam of light coming from the ceiling and covering the table top? That's where Peter is standing. There, in that beam of light. He came back to tell me things he wants me to know about my future. Alex, it was amazing. Peter took me through every second of our life together. It was thrilling to see how we lived and all the things we did. I loved doing it all over, again. After that, he insisted he needed to talk to you."

Pointing at Liz, Alex asks, "Liz? Are you all right? Can I get you anything? Can I help you somehow? Liz?"

Laughing, Liz answers. "No, Alex, I don't need anything. I'm more than alright. Look, there in the center of the dining table, don't you see Peter within the beam of light coming down from the ceiling? It lights the entire table and Peter's right in the center watching both of us. Beside him are two other people. I'm sure Peter will tell me about them after he's talked to you. He said they came back to talk with my others, but I don't know what he meant by that. Right now, he says to tell you to sit next to me and be quiet. Listen to what I am saying as Peter will talk to you through me. He says I won't hear what he tells you."

Wide eyed, Alex stares at Liz and asks, "Liz? Have you gone nuts? Peter's dead. How could he come back here and be standing on top of your table?"

Liz points at the table, "Alex, Peter's in that beam of light. Don't tell me you don't see the light beam? Look. There. We're only a few feet from him."

"No, Liz, no. There is nothing on the table. Not Peter nor anybody else." Alex shouts as she runs to the table and slaps her hands across the top causing the beam of light to vanish. "Do you see anything now?

There's nothing on this table and there wasn't before. Not Peter. Not a beam of light. Not any other people. There is nothing on the table, Liz!"

Liz rushes to Alexandria and pulls the angry woman back to the sofa. "Don't do that, Alex. Sit and be quiet. Hush. All you did was cause the light to disappear. Now it'll be a while before Peter comes back. Don't worry though, he said he has an important message for you so I'm sure he'll return soon."

Alex slowly returns to Liz and stares at her as if seeing her for the first time. "Good God, Liz, you've gone over the edge. You are absolutely crazy."

Laughing, Liz shakes her head and replies, "No, Alex, no, I'm not crazy. I'm simply amazed by it all and you will be, too. Peter will come back and speak to you. There. See the beam of light? Now do you see him in there? Peter's the one in front. You must see him. He's in the middle of the table. I told you he'd return. Of course, Alex, I know it's not Peter, but, yes, somehow, it is Peter. It's his essence, his soul or whatever you want to call it. I'm sure once he's told us all he needs us to know, he'll leave and be gone forever."

"Liz, you must not imagine such things. Peter is dead. You know that. If you don't stop this, you'll go mad."

"Of course, he's dead, Alex. I know that better than you do. Peter was cremated and I spread his ashes on the outgoing tide this morning. But he has come back to tell us both something he wants us to know. Now hush. Peter says to be silent while he talks to you through me. I'll be asleep when he does, as his words are for you only. So listen to his words when I say them for you."

"What did you say, Liz?" Alex demands. "What are you trying to do to me? I have nothing to say to your dead husband, Peter. Why are you doing this? Damn it to hell, I'm telling you, Liz, Peter is not here!"

Suddenly, Liz shouts at Alex, "Yes, Alex, I am here. I tell you to shut up and listen to what I tell you. All is known of you and those around you." At that moment, Liz closes her eyes and she hears no more of what Peter tells Alex. Only when she is shaken awake several minutes later, does Liz's hearing return.

Alexandria Petrow is yelling at her, "Liz. Liz, I saw him. I saw Peter in the beam of light. He was as you said he was. There were two people with him. Damn it, Liz, the light is so bright, I have to squint. Damn him to hell. Peter knew it all, everything, about me and the work I do for others. He knew it the whole time I lived here. Did you know about me, too, Liz? Liz? Wake up, Liz, damn you, wake up right now. Damn you to hell." Alex yells as she slaps Liz several times on her arms with the last blow across the face.

Pushing her away, Liz cries out, "Stop, Alex. Stop hitting me, damn it. That hurts. I'm awake and I heard you say you saw Peter and the two others with him. You did say that, didn't you, Alex? You saw Peter? I can tell you did, Alex. And he's scared you for some reason. Why are you so frightened, Alex? What Peter? He says you're to leave here, right now. He says you are to go home and choose wisely. Live or die, the choice is yours. Go away and live or stay and die. My goodness, Peter, those are harsh words. Why would you say that to Alex? You know she's my friend."

Alex stares at Liz and asks, "You heard what Peter said to me?"

"Yes, after you woke me up. At this time. I did. He's telling me now to tell you to go home. I didn't hear what he said to you while I slept. At that time, he spoke directly to you. You saw him talking to you, didn't you? Ouch, Alex! Let go of my hand. You're hurting me. Stop, Alex! Why are you hurting me? Why are you so frightened? What did Peter say to scare you so badly?"

"To hell with you and your damned Peter." Alexandria Petrow shouts as she stands and throws Liz's hand back at her. "Yes, I see that dead husband of yours and the two others behind him in a beam of light. Yes, I see the two rooms tied to yours where those others of you live. And, now, I say for you all to go straight to hell," Without another word, Alex rushes out the open slider door and vanishes into the stormy night.

Suddenly, Peter's voice fills her head, *'Alexandria Petrow was never your friend. Give her space and time to flee. I repeat, Elizabeth Ann Anderson Day, Alexandria Petrow was never your friend. Now, it is time to meet your others.'*

Liz frowns. "My others? Peter, you keep saying that. What do you mean by my 'others'? Aren't the man and woman with you, those others?"

'No, those were known by your Parallel Lives during their lifetimes, as we knew each other in ours. Your others are the two women the people, in the beam of light with me, knew in their last life. You and your others were born as one entity named Elizabeth Ann Anderson. The women are of that same life as are you. Each of you are Parallel Lives from that one entity. The only difference is when and why you each split from that life. Watch them and wait. You will soon know them soon as their dimensions overlap yours, thus your homes are tied together. Meet with them at the focused point of the glowing stone under the adjoined dining tables. This translucent agate, set in the floor of your Dad's original cabin, is the adjoined point of your childhood which each of you shared. Each Elizabeth Ann Anderson is a Parallel Life of the original Elizabeth Ann Anderson.

FIVE

June 5—The Others

PETER'S image vanishes from within the beam of light. However, the images behind him become clear to Liz. The red-haired man's anger is so strong towards the woman he faces that he punches out of the light beam as if trying to reach her. The woman does not notice him as she reads her book in front of the stone fireplace and sips from her glass of wine. The fire in the fireplace flickers with a low flame and Liz realizes the fireplace has been updated to use propane.

From where Liz sits, she also sees each stone of her own fireplaces fit exactly over the ones in the other space. There is a narrow black table behind the white sofa which holds a reading lamp at each end and a few books. The wine glass, from which the woman sips, is where the woman can reach it when she turns to her left. There is a dining table that overlaps Liz's table and is directly over the translucent agate that glows within the dark stain of the polished cement floor. "Wow I like that look. Maybe it's time to redo my own floor."

When the red-haired man in the beam of light can't get the attention of the woman he faces, he becomes frantic and tears at his silk robe until it hangs in shreds from his body. When that happens, the woman looks up from her book and reaches over the back of the sofa to pick up a remote off the sofa table. Aiming the remote across the room, the woman clicks it and Kenny G's saxophone dances through the room. The woman smiles as she sets the remote back where it was.

Then as if suddenly seeing something new, the woman looks to where Liz sits at the dining table, in front of the west windows. When a puzzled expression settles on the woman's face, Liz expects the woman to speak to her. However, the woman gives a hard quick shake of her head, picks up her book and reads.

Stunned by this mutual moment of recognition, Liz sees the woman's face is exactly as her own. Their eyes, noses, chins, cheekbones and the mouths areas as if cloned from one person. Topping everything, is the prematurely white hair each has. The only differences, which Liz can see, are the style of their hair and the fact that the other woman is ten pounds heavier.

"My God, Peter, if the woman lost ten pounds and cut her hair as short as mine, no one could tell us apart. I don't understand this, Peter, who is she and why does that man hate her so much? Why did you bring them to me at this time?"

At that moment, the beam of light darkens to a deep orange and Liz hears the man scream horribly. Frightened, Liz runs from the table to sit in the corner of her own sofa. Peter's speaks to her, *'Do not be afraid. He can no longer harm her or any others. His fierce anger rebounds back to him as if lightning striking solid stone. Each time, it is twice as powerful. Though he cringes from each bolt, his hate is too complete. The Omnipresent Omnipotent Universal Energy Force has intervened to humble and control him. His negatives are too many and they have erased her one negative act of killing him though not the other with him.*

While Peter speaks, Liz is blinded by a brilliant flash that knocks the red-haired man onto his knees. Then the light darkens to a deep red glow and there is another flash of light. When Liz is able to see again, only the young black woman stands within the beam of light. The angry man is gone.

Liz gasps. "Peter? What happened to that man?"

His negative karma returned him to the Universal Plain as he must evolve into a life which he will experience that which he gave in this life. If he does not learn from that life lesson, he will repeat the experience until he accepts lesson with unconditional love. When the life lesson has been learned, he will enjoy a humble, loving life, with others who care for him. See, the woman turns down the music as he is gone. Though she did not hear or see the man, his negative force was felt by her and she responds to his leaving.

At that, the woman on the white leather sofa fades from Liz's view and the young black woman is the only figure within the light beam. The beautiful woman leans forward reaching out to the woman sitting on the old brown leather sofa sitting to the right of the stone fireplace which is the same as the other two fireplaces. The brown leather sofa overlaps Liz's black leather swing chairs which sit to that side of the room and the woman, with the ponytail, sits at the far end away from Liz. At first the woman does not notice the young black woman within the beam of light on the tabletop.

The dark lovely woman seems about to leap from the light beam and join the woman on the old sofa. This room is much the same as Liz's, yet has a difference which Liz recognizes immediately and she whispers, "Peter, this cabin is the same as my Dad's cabin. The same as ours was before we took out the bedroom to add the stairs to the top floor. Everything is how I remember it. It's as if I've stepped back in time. That old leather sofa and its matching club chairs, are the same as I remember. The end tables and lamps are different. However, the dining table is the same as mine and the other one. It's as if I went back to being a kid again and, look Peter, look how much I look like the woman on the old sofa and she looks like me, in every way except our hair. Cut off her long ponytailed hair and we'd look as if we'd been cloned."

As Liz studies the two women, she nods, "You are right, Peter, those women are of me or I am of them. How can we exist in this space and never have known each other? You said we live in separate dimensions.

If this is so, how will we ever meet? Aren't dimensions other worlds separate from each other?"

Instead of an answer, the beam of light disappears and, at that moment, the floors and ceilings of the three homes mesh together and the three dining tables become adjoined to one another as if one house.

SIX

June 5—Beth

BETH shakes with anger as she watches her sister, Dee, turn her car onto Shoreline Drive and disappears around the south curve. Beth fumes, "That damned, bitch. No wonder her twins fled from Dee as soon as they could and Ed's divorcing her. Please, let this be the last time I have to tell her that the cabin doesn't belong to me anymore. The State of Washington owns all of Redcliff's Beach and the cabin. I get to live here till I die or the place washes out from under me."

As she enters the carport, a stiff gust of wind hits her hard and she stumbles back a step. Righting herself, Beth looks up at the sky. "Better get the deck chairs tucked into the carport, Max. Those black clouds look as if they're carrying quite a load this time. We could use a good drenching to break the long drought we've been having this summer." Suddenly she stops and laughs. "Oh good lord, I'm talking to myself. Maxine, I miss you so much. I'd better get a pet to follow me around so when I talk to myself, people will think I'm talking to it. Either that or let them haul me to the loony bin where Dee spends most of her time."

After the last of the deck furniture is in the carport, wind gusts hit the side of the cabin and with it comes a pounding rain. The waves smash onto the narrow strip of sand and roll up around the cabin. A bit frightened, Beth realizes it will be the first storm she'll face since Maxine's death. When bolts of lightning streak across the sky, she shakes her fist at the flashes and yells, "Here it comes, Max. It's not a good day on Redcliff's Beach. First, that damn Dee shows up and berates me for giving away the cabin. The stupid selfish bitch didn't say one kind word about you or your death. All she did was demand the State turn it over to Nicole and Nancy.

"Dad told me years ago that 'we have no control over the family we're born into, or the nuts that come with it, therefore choose friends with great care as they're the ones who become true family.' And with that thought, I need to call the Sheriff and report that my sister, the family nut, Dee, has violated the injunction not to come within a mile of me or the cabin. I hope this is the last time I ever have to do it."

Walking to the kitchen counter, Beth sits on a stool and uses her cellphone to call the Sheriff. She quickly explains about Dee threatening her and the Deputy says not to worry. His contact at the Oregon Patrol will send someone to look for her. This time, Dee will be booked and may have some jail time.

Satisfied things will move in the right direction, Beth fixes a sandwich for lunch and takes the plate to the dining table. Directly in front of her, in the center of the table, sits the platter of shells with the large pink snail shell she'd given to Maxine the day she died. Beth holds it for several minutes before she sets it back with the other shells and wipes her eyes.

At that moment, the large book lying to the left of the seashells causes her to smile. It's the last gift Maxine bought for her and the last gift Beth had unwrapped last Christmas morning. The book was one of those things which Beth had talked about buying but always thought it was much too expensive to buy for herself and was very pleased that Maxine remembered and gave it to her.

The atlas sized tome, "METAPHYSICAL MOMENTS THAT COULD HAPPEN TO YOU" was three inches thick and weighed five pounds. "Not exactly a book to read in bed," Beth chuckles as she takes a bite of her sandwich before she opens the large cover and lays each page over until she comes to the table of contents. Turning to the first chapter, she feels a bit guilty as she knows Maxine never liked her to read while she ate. However, things are different now and reading at any time helps keep her loneliness in check.

When there is a lull in the storm, she hears a soft voice asking a question. Puzzled, Beth looks around the room and, though she doesn't see anyone, she asks, "Were you speaking to me?" The soft voice repeats the question, "Hello there, do you hear me?"

Frowning, Beth answers, "Yes I do. Where are you?"

The voice answers, "Over on the sofa. I'm Elizabeth Ann Anderson Day. Is that your name?"

Beth answers, "Yes. I'm Elizabeth Ann Anderson. Dee? Is that you? What sort of trick are you trying to pull? What are you doing here? Where are you?" Sitting very still, the only sound Beth hears is the storm whipping around the corner of the cabin. Angry, Beth pushes away from the table and checks each room as she looks for her sister. When she finds no one, she returns to the table, the sandwich and the book.

While she reads, a soft glow of light begins to cover the table. At first the light reaches the plate of shells, then it covers the book's pages and Beth stands up and walks to the kitchen taking the empty dish with her. From behind the kitchen counter, she watches as the light brightens. Squinting to see, she looks up at the ceiling where she knows there is no light fixture. "What the hell is going on here? There's no light in that ceiling. What the hell is going on?" Backing away, she watches the light blend with the light from the agate set in the floor under the table. When the two become so brilliant that she can't watch it, she runs to her bedroom and slams the door.

After several minutes, Beth begins to feel foolish about being so frightened by the light. Opening the bedroom door, she sees the light has vanished and decides she saw some form of static electricity from the storm. Walking to the table, she picks up the heavy book and carries it to the club chair which faces the fireplace and turns on the reading lamp on the end table.

After she opens the large book, she reads for several minutes before she notices the room has become very bright. Looking up, Beth sees the beam of light coming from the ceiling over the dining table. As she looks into the light, she sees a shape moving within it and the agate in the floor is pulsing in a tempo with the light from above.

As the pulsing lights dim, Beth sees the shape is a person. Shocked, Beth shouts, "Max? Maxine? Is that you? Am I going mad? It can't be you so I must be mad. Oh dear God, what is this? Why are you doing this to me?"

Unable to stop herself, Beth walks over to the table and circles it several times. As she does, a woman becomes visible within the light and moves with Beth. When Beth stops close to the table, the woman's image reaches out to Beth and Beth grabs the hands offered. Instantly, the image and beam of light vanish.

Rushing back to her chair, Beth stares at the table and begins to weep. Through her tears, she sees the glow under the table brighten and she cries out, "Maxine? Please come back. I'll behave, I won't touch you. Please come back. Please."

As if an answer, the light drops from the ceiling, onto the table top, and widens until it covers the long table. While it does, the stone under the table shimmers a soft gold. It is then that Beth sees the form within the light beam has taken a solid shape and knows, without a doubt, that it is Maxine. "Maxine, Maxine, You came back. Oh, Max. What? How? Why are you here? Was it you who spoke earlier? Was that you? Max?"

This Maxine is young and more beautiful than Beth had ever known her to be. This beautiful woman moves gracefully within the beam of light as she reaches her arms out as if to touch Beth. Crying with joy, Beth walks to the side of the table and exclaims, "Darling, it is you, you're here. You are here. You're younger and more beautiful than I have ever known you. When we met that first day in the Graduate Library, we were both so exhausted from our long hours of research for our PhDs. Never were you as young as you are now. Never was I. By the time we finished our degrees, we were the full-bodied women we stayed for the rest of our lifetimes."

As Beth talks, this young Maxine sways gently as if to some soft music and smiles tenderly at Beth. The woman's face is so filled with compassion that Beth feels as if her heart will burst. When the image holds her hands out, Beth reaches into the light and takes hold of the hands.

In that instant, the light and the image vanish and the room becomes dark. Stunned, Beth backs away until she sits on the club chair. Tears flood down her cheeks as she stares at the top of the table. She does not move and is almost afraid to breathe. Several minutes pass before the agate in the floor glows bright and is joined by light from the ceiling. When these lights brighten, Beth sees the essence of Maxine Oakley is centered on the table.

Unable to move, Beth watches from her chair. Then her mind is filled with Maxine's words. *'Darling Beth. I am here with you one more time. My darling, feel my love and gratitude. You were always there for me. You were the best to happen to me in my lifetime. I feel your grief. Mourn no more. Let go of your pain and feel the joy we shared together. Release the pain, Beth, Mourn no more, my darling.*

'You were my joy, my true love. I give you my thanks and my gratitude. Stay well. Be happy. You will come when it is your time, not sooner. Till then, know my love continues. Love will come to you in many forms, in future years. Others come who are of you. Do not be afraid. Greet them as they are of you and you are of them. You will meet them soon. Be comforted by them. You will love them as the family they are. A youth needs your love and guidance. Take her into your heart as she needs you more than ever.'

As Maxine's voice fills her mind, Beth wipes her eyes with the backs of her hands and snuffles. "I can't help crying, Maxine. You know I always cry when I'm happy and I'm so happy, Max, I'm so happy you are with me again. You're so beautiful. It's such a joy to see you healthy and young, my dearest. Thank you for giving me this image of you. It's wonderful." Again, unable to stop herself, Beth walks to the table and reaches for Maxine's extended hands. Again, the beam of light vanishes, taking Maxine with it.

"I'll stop doing that, Max. Please come back to me. Please, I don't want to lose you. Not tonight. Please. Come back one more time," Beth pleads as she waits on one of the chairs by the dining table for the light to bring Maxine back to her. After several minutes, she walks to the slider door and looks out at the raging storm. "What if she doesn't return? No, I won't think about that. She must come back, she must, please, Max, please... I won't touch you again. I'll behave."

As she stares out the glass slider, a reflected glow lights the room behind her and Beth turns to see the light dancing upon the table. Without a word, Beth sinks onto one of the chairs next to the table. This time, when the youthful Maxine reappears within the beam of light, Beth takes the silk throw off Maxine's bentwood rocker, wraps it around her hips, then, strutting to the table, she claps her hands. Then, with a toss of her head, she laughs as she's not laughed for months. To Beth's delight, Maxine responds with the same toss of her head and clapping of her hands. Whooping with delight, Beth swirls the wrap around her hips and stamps her feet dancing as they learned on a long ago trip through Spain. Beth's sparkling blue eyes never leave the flash of Maxine's auburn ones as the two women respond and repeat to every move the other makes.

Though time seems to stand still, hours pass as the two move in tandem to music only they hear. The storm whips around the cabin without interrupting their last connection, Beth is too entranced to notice anything but the joy in Maxine's face and the love in her own heart. As the women dance through the night, the fury of the storm slowly dies away with the dawn.

The sun cracks over the Coastal Mountain Range and colors the western horizon. It is then that the beam of light begins to fade into the new day and Maxine goes with it. Watching Maxine disappear, Beth says, "You were everything to me, Maxine, my love, my joy, my very life. Goodbye, my darling."

I am called to other places for other purposes. Know our love is eternal, Beth. I kiss your lips forever.

SEVEN

June 5—Eliza

ELIZA is setting her dinner dishes into the dishwasher when there is a loud knocking on the front door. Then, the doorbell chimes several times in rapid succession, after which the hard knocking begins again. Crossing to the entry doors, Eliza checks the security monitor and sees a familiar face looming within its frame. Even though the person is looking up at the security camera. Eliza shouts into the intercom, "Who the hell's out there and what do you want?"

"Eliza? Mrs. Staples? Eliza? Frank Gilbert, here. Sheriff Gilbert? Jack's friend from Hood River. Yours, too? Open the door, I need a talk with you." Looking at the face on the monitor, she tells herself, *'Now it begins. I know nothing. Remember. I know nothing. I know nothing.'*

Turning the bolt, Eliza pulls open the carved door and Frank Gilbert lumbered into the home. When he sees her, his frown turns into a smile that gives a hint of how handsome he'd been at some point in his lifetime.

Eliza growls, "Frank, what the hell are you doing, trying to break down my door? Most people ring the bell once or twice or use the knocker with a light touch. Just look at you, you're soaked. Take off that leather jacket and I'll hang it over by the fireplace screen."

As she speaks, Eliza moves ahead to where she'll hang the jacket. When she hears the door slam, she turns to watch the big man come to where she waits. After he hands her his wet jacket, Eliza drapes the soggy leather over one side of the ornate screen in front of the low flames flickering within the propane fireplace.

"Sit on the sofa and warmup in front of the fireplace. I'll get a towel so you can dry off. What in the world brings you out on a night like this?" Talking as she walks into the kitchen, she hears him mumbles something and calls back, "Don't talk yet, I can't hear you. Wait until I get back with your coffee." As she fills a large mug, Eliza's mind whirls as she repeats over and over, '*I know nothing, I know nothing, I know nothing...*'

Returning to where Frank waits on the sofa, she sets the tray with the mugs on the narrow low table in front of him and tosses a bath towel to him. "Dry off, then drink up while the coffee's hot. I assumed you still take three sugars and cream. Right?"

"Yeah, Eliza, it's fine." Frank Gilbert nods. "Thanks. Now, sit with me and I'll tell you why I'm here. It's real serious, Eliza. Wouldn't come all this way on a lark."

"My God, Frank, you're giving me chills." Eliza shivers and hugs her shoulders. "Did the company burn down? The mansion? Did Jack total another car? It's all right, Frank, tell me. I'm a strong woman."

Taking a deep breath, Gilbert sighs, "Hell, there's no easy way to say this Eliza, Jack's dead. Your maid, Lisa, found him this morning."

"Jack's dead? Did he fall down the stairs again? Drunk?" Eliza chokes out a half laugh then sobs. "For God sakes, Frank, tell me what happened." Tears spill down her cheeks. "Shit, I've hated that sorry son of a bitch for the past twenty years and now I'm crying over his puny ass. Go figure."

"Eliza, not another word till I finish. First off, it weren't no accident. Was murder. Someone killed him in the Mansion. Shot him three times. He weren't alone. Peg Hartman were killed, too. She's your friend, right? Hell, Eliza, she were blowing him. Yah know? On your bed. That's where we found them. Both naked and dead. Peg were shot once at back of her head. Jack shot three times. You understanding me, Eliza?"

"No. Frank, I'm not following what you're saying. I don't understand how it could be Peg. She's my best friend. She told me just a week ago how much she hated Jack for the way he treated me. Said he was a shit to be with all those women. Besides, why the hell were they in my bedroom? Frank? Peg couldn't stand to be in the same room with him. Oh, dear God, does Mike Hartman know? He'll be down in Chili at this time of year on a fruit sales trip. He's the company's top salesman. Have you told him? Was it a robbery?" Suddenly, Eliza stops talking and gasps for breath, visibly shaken.

Frank Gilbert lifts a woolen throw off the back of the sofa and lays it gently across Eliza's shoulders. "No, we can't find Mike. Seems he left Chili for New York days ago. Don't think it were him as it looks to be a contract killing. Were Jack gambling again? Know his big problem last year. Got in deep in Vegas and left town without paying up. Remember?"

Frowning at Gilbert's remark, as she exclaims, "No, Frank, I don't remember Jack gambling, last year or ever. Are you sure about that? Why that dumb bastard. No wonder he pawed around the company's accounts when he thought nobody was looking."

"You didn't hear of Jack's close call last year? Guess it's time you did. Story he told me, he lost a million of some casino's money, then left Vegas without paying up. That crash he had last year? Weren't no accident. A couple of toughs came up to collect. Then took him for a ride. Said he sold his Staples stock to you as only way he could get the fast cash. Sure you didn't know?"

"No, Frank, Jack asked for money to invest in some company. He didn't have any stock to sell to me or anyone else. I gave him a large sum that took him off the Company's accounts except his Sales accounts. He worked for every penny he had until he took over as President when I retired. It was a business venture that later went sour and everything fell through. The board put him back on salary when he stepped into my old position." Eliza laughs, a bit too loudly, and shakes her head. "Poor old Jack. No wonder he whined about being broke all the time. He really didn't have any money. Frank, that's is just too sad for words."

Eliza frowns at Gilbert and says, "But, you knew, Frank. You, his best friend, you knew Jack was in deep. Why didn't you tell me? You knew he never would. As his friend, Frank, you should have told me. We could have gotten him help. I know Jack and I hadn't really been together for over twenty years, but together we could have helped him. I was never surprised at anything Jack did. Even now, I'm not surprised when you tell me he took his woman to my bed. That's Jack. However, Peg? Peg betray me? Why would she do that to me? How long have they been involved? Did she gamble, too?"

"Not that we know, Eliza. Frank got wild these last years. I never hung with him much. I got a sweet wife. Wouldn't hurt her for the world. Yeah, I once ran with Jack. He were like a brother. These last years, just off and on." Frank pauses and stares into the fireplace as tears fill his eyes. "Just a shit way to go, that's what I say. A real shit way to go."

Neither Eliza nor Frank speak for several minutes. As Frank stares into the fireplace, Eliza watches his face change from one emotion after another until he clears his throat and she looks away. "Sorry, Eliza, got lost for a moment. Hell, enough of this, let me finish about the house. Nothing seems out of place. Were clothes scattered at the front door with a small suitcase. Jack's car there, too, with the doors open the battery run down. You'll have to tell what's missing. Don't look so, but till you look, we won't know for certain.

"Here's what we're thinking happened," he continues. "Jack and Peg came in his Mercedes. Got passionate in the front seat. Got undressed going through front doors. Figure Jack turned off house alarm then. Moved upstairs to your room. Were a half bottle of champagne with two full glasses near the bed, but the cork were in a towel by the kitchen sink with the glassware cabinet open. We figure he'd gone downstairs to get wine and took it back up. He must've felt safe enough, as the front door was wide open as clothes and the small case kept it open. When your maid, Lisa, got back from vacation trip Jack paid for. She went to Mexico to see her family. Came home yesterday, she says. I'm thinking Jack got her out of his way. That way, she didn't catch him and Peg in the act. That's my thoughts, not her statement. Like I said, the alarm was turned off. We figure that made Jack easy picking for who did the job.

"Your maid took it real hard. She's in the hospital. Wants you to come see her, when you get back. I told her, I'd give you the message. It's a hell of a mess, Eliza, a hell of a mess. Geez, the town never had such a mess. Most figured he'd be killed by some cuckolded hubby. Like you said, was Peg's being there that stunned everyone. Jack pushed both ends to the middle and this time, he got real burnt.

"Need you to come back with me to get things settled, Eliza. Need your fingerprints to check off from those we found. Also, a statement of when you last saw Jack and Peg. Everyone, who knew them, is doing this. Mike Hartman will do it, when we find him. You go get your things and we'll get going. Could you do it now?"

"What? Now? No. No, Frank, not tonight. I'm not going with you nor am I driving myself anywhere tonight. No, Frank, give me one night to take this all in. I realize that Jack wasn't much of a husband, but he was Mina's son and she loved him. We were together for thirty years. I only divorced him this spring as I didn't want anything he did to intrude into my new life here. Damn it, Frank, I need time to think this over. No, I'll come over tomorrow. That's soon enough. Yes, I'll go tomorrow. I'll let you know when I get to my sister's as that's where I'll stay. I'll call you then. Right now, I need to phone my sister, Marie and Mike and Staples' lawyers and have the Chairman of the Board appoint a new President for the company. That's what I'm going to do tonight, Frank. I'll be there tomorrow. Now go away, Frank. Please leave. I need to be alone. Please, just go away."

"Don't know if I should leave you, Eliza. Hate you to drive yourself back there."

"Leave me alone, Frank, I'll come there tomorrow. I am shaken and terribly sad by what you've told me. Right now, all I want to do is make my phone calls then lie down and think. Please, go away. I need to make sense out of Peggy's betrayal. How could she do this to me? All those years, she was my good friend? Frank? Why did she betray me with Jack?"

Tears run down Eliza's cheeks and she abruptly stands. Without another word, she lifts Frank's jacket off the fireplace screen and holds it out to him. As Frank puts it on, he says, "I got reports to make, Eliza. If you're not coming, get a clean glass and hold it with both hands. That way, forensics can start identifying fingerprints. You can't go to the mansion, Eliza. It's been sealed. You need things from it? I go with you. Sorry. But, that's how it's got to be."

"Then, you'll do it, Frank. There're only a few things I want from that house. You send someone over tomorrow to bag Jack's personal items from his drawers and closets. Give them to Goodwill or put them somewhere on the first floor. Have someone you trust do it, I'll pay for their services. I will want to empty the safe in a day or two and secure the house for a future estate sale. Take the bed and bedding out of my room, as soon as you can. Everything else is gone or up here. Don't tell me it isn't your job, Frank. As Jack's friend, knowing what you did, and didn't do, you owe me that and much more. Damn it! Why couldn't Jack have gotten himself killed in his own bed or outside of the house?"

EIGHT

June 10—Liz

LIZ calls from Peter's desk phone to leave a message asking Bob Drake what the FAA decided caused Peter's plane crash. After that, she walks out to the kitchen and sees other dining tables have adjoined to her own table. Puzzled, she goes to the table and watches for the other women. Suddenly, the women are standing within an open glass slider door. The ponytailed one is coming inside while the other one seems to be going outside. When Liz sees them, they are facing each other in the doorway. Both have puzzled looks on their faces as they stare at the woman in front of them.

So pleased to see both of them at once, Liz calls out, "Hi there, I see you two have met. I'm so glad to find you both here today. Will you come and sit at your tables and talk with me? You must know by now, that we were all named Elizabeth Ann Anderson at birth and our parents were James and Jill Anderson. We have a sister named Dana Marie. I'm known as Liz Day and my sister is Dana Hall. Would you tell me the names you use now?"

Neither of the women respond to her questions as if they don't hear her and are still staring at the woman in their way. Irritated, Liz shouts,

"Hey you two. Come to your tables and sit with me. My late husband, Peter, told me our phenomenon is called Parallel Lives and we each are from one child named Elizabeth Ann Anderson. He said we are to know each other soon for we are Parallel Lives."

As neither woman turns to her, Liz decides the other two women are unaware of her. However, the ponytailed woman pushes past the other woman and stops next to the dining table. Glaring at Liz, she demands, "Who the hell are you to shout at me? How did you get into my home? I don't understand why you think you can order me around. Take your friend and both of you get out of my home. Now."

Taking a step towards Liz, she is grabbed by the woman she'd pushed from the doorway. Screaming at the ponytailed woman, the woman twists the hand she holds, "Who are you? Who the hell are you? Where did you come from? What are you doing in my home?"

The ponytailed woman, cries out, "Let go of me. Let go. You're hurting me. I want you both out of my house right now. I said let go of me, right now!"

This interaction of the two women delights Liz and she tells them, "Stop, both of you. Stop and look at each other. Don't you see how much you look like each other? Look at me. I'm the same as you both. The only difference is the way our hair is cut. We are Parallel Lives from one child named Elizabeth Ann Anderson.

"When we were this child, we came here with our family to stay in this cabin our Dad built. Our name is Elizabeth Ann Anderson, the name of the original child. One of us might even be that one child, though we won't know until we talk with each other to find out what memories we have in common and at what age those joined memories stop. Please, come sit at our adjoined tables. We have to talk. It's the only way we will know who we are."

The ponytailed woman lets the arm of the third woman drop and frowns at Liz, "What in the hell are you talking about? This is my home and you are both intruders. I want you out of here. Both of you. Go."

When her hand is freed, the third woman pushes the ponytailed woman away and says, "Your house? This is my home. It was my Dad's cabin and I've remodeled it and moved up to live fulltime. My sister, Marie, and I remodeled the inside and added two floors up those stairs where the bedroom was. You two get out of here. You're trespassers and I don't want you in here."

The woman, with the ponytail, points at the woman and shouts, "I know who you are. I've seen you before. You ran through my home the day Maxine died. I followed you when you ran through my slider door and out the front door. How did you get in here again? What do you want from me?"

Before either woman could say more, Liz yells, "Stop bickering. Look at each other. Look at me. We're exactly like each other. We're each from one child. We're each Elizabeth Ann Andersons. I'm now called Liz Day. What are your names? Please stop fussing about who, how and why. Look at each other. You must see how exactly alike we are.

"See how our dining tables have meshed together? We're each in our own homes in separate dimensions. I don't know what to make of this anymore than you do. However, I feel certain that the only way we will understand is to sit together and talk. Maybe we can come to understand this paradox that ties us together. I need to know what has happened. Please, let's talk together. Please."

Moving around to the side of the table, Liz points to the glowing stone in the floor and says, "My table sits over the translucent agate my Dad put into his cabin's concrete floor. I played around that stone all the while I was little. So did my sister, Dana. Dad's name was James Anderson and Mom's name was Jill. Did you both have a sister named Dana Marie?"

The two women stare at Liz. Then, the ponytailed woman asks, "Your Dad built your cabin at a Redcliff's Beach? Did you race your sister Dana down the beach to be first to slap your touchstone at the red cliffs and shout 'I declare this run good and done.'"

"Yes to everything you said," yelps Liz. "Oh yes. Please come sit and talk with me."

As the woman sits in a chair close to Liz, she turns to the third woman still standing in the open slider door and says, "Don't run away. Come over here and sit with us. I agree with Liz, we three need to talk about this strange paradox we find ourselves within. We must try to understand what caused our dimensions to overlap and how we came to be."

Without answering, the third woman moves from the open doorway to the edge of her dining table. Frowning, she runs her hands over the table's smooth surface until she touches the edge where it overlaps the two other tables. At that moment, her frown fades as she rubs her hands over the odd area. "It feels as if electricity is flowing in this spot and I feel a sort of humming or vibration. What do you think happened that brought us together?"

Liz says, "I feel strongly that it is at this place where Dad set the agate into the floor that connects us. I'm Liz Day. What are your names?"

The ponytailed woman smiles, "I'm Elizabeth Ann Anderson, too, Liz. Now, I'm called Beth Anderson. My cabin is the same as Dad's cabin was except that my partner, Maxine, and I added a laundry to the bathroom and a guest room both on the uphill side. Then we covered the space out front for a carport over the entrance. My partner of thirty years, Maxine Oakley, died of ovarian cancer two weeks ago, on the first of June at two in the afternoon."

Liz gasps, "My husband Peter died in a plane crash on Mt. Michael on June first. One of the rescuers told me that when they reached him, he was still alive. He passed away after they tried to move him from the plane around two that afternoon."

When she says that, the woman with the shoulder length hair, shouts at her, "Don't say that. Don't. It can't be true. What are you trying to do to me? How could you both have someone die on that exact date and time? What are you trying to do to me? I won't tell you what I did. I won't. I can't. I can't."

Instantly, Beth stands and takes the woman into arms and holds her. When this happens, both women vanish and Liz is alone in her own home at her own table. The two other women have vanished.

Standing, Liz rushes around to where the women had stood even though she knows they are gone, she looks out the open door to see if they were on the deck or on the beach. They are nowhere to be seen. Turning to the north window, she sees Alex's house and remembers the night Peter came back to warn her about her old friend.

"I've got to clear out Peter's things and empty that office. I'll move my things into it. Maybe I'll find that book Alex wanted. I still doubt Peter would ever borrow anything of hers."

As she thinks of how much Peter disliked Alex, Liz wonders, "Did he protest too much? I wasn't with them every second, so who knows what went on between those two." Saying that, she remembers Peter's caution about Alex and her jangled nerves when her neighbor was seen at his office door.

Walking towards the office door, she hears her name and turns to see the woman called Beth at the adjoined tables. Liz quickly joins her at the tables and the two sit silently studying the other.

It is Beth who speaks first, "Yes, Liz, I was born Elizabeth Ann Anderson and am now Beth Anderson. Maxine and I were both lesbians and declared our love thirty years ago in front of family, friends and God. Even though same sex marriages weren't legal back then, we made legal commitments to each other that bound us more than a legal marriage would have done.

"When I hugged the other woman to calm her, she vanished at the same time you did. I agree that the only way we will ever know what or who we are is to talk together as often as we can. Let's try to meet here every morning. You said you run most mornings, could you meet me here afterwards? I'd love to have a set time to be with you."

Without moving, Liz answers, "Yes, that would be great, Beth. I want to know you and I hope we'll get to know the other woman also. My dead husband Peter returned last week. He came back in a beam of light and told me there were three of us. We lived within separate dimensions, though each of us lives in Dad's cabin and each cabin has the large agate under these tables. That's the proof of our connection and the reason our tables are now adjoined."

Beth smiles as she walks to sit beside Liz, "The Summer Solstice will be here in a couple weeks. We must meet the other woman by that time. Maybe her seeing us in her home will help her get used to us by then. Right now, I really need to give you a hug and if we vanish to our own homes, I'll see you tomorrow, my friend."

Liz smiles at Beth as the two wrap their arms around the other and hold on for several seconds before each vanishes from the other's home. Not surprised, Liz tells herself, "One thing for sure, Beth and I have made a good connection. However, as I said before, I need to get Peter's office cleaned out and make it mine. I'm sure Bob Drake needs papers in there in order to close down Peter's share of their business."

When she stops at Peter's office door, she gives the handle a twist to open it and finds it locked. Frowning, she stares at the knob, then chuckles, "Okay, Peter, where's the key? Is Alex's book really in there? Is she why he always locked the door? Maybe he'd found her inside on days I was traveling. Maybe he saw how curious she was about what he did.

"I, on the other hand, always left the slider door unlocked until that one day. Alex could have come over any of those mornings and found Peter's office locked. Damn it, Peter, where did you put that key? More importantly, why lock a door unless there's stuff you don't want people to see?"

When those last words leave her tongue, Liz's mind whirls with many possibilities. "Were you and Bob dealing with things illegal or immoral? Huh, Peter, love of my life? What were you two up to, old buddy of mine? What didn't you want anyone, even me, to go inside during your trips? You certainly never meant to die on a mountain top."

Suddenly, something Peter said to her the morning of his crash slips into her mind and Liz whispers, "I thought it was odd when you took me into your arms and whispered in my ear that to remember that if I ever had to hide anything 'to always hide it in plain sight.'"

The memory stops her and she rethinks his statement, "Peter, you were telling me that you hid things in plain sight or a place you used often. I think I know where you meant, my clever friend."

Hurrying into the mudroom, she goes to the row of pegs along the wall which have several jackets hanging off them. Lifting the ancient 'flack-jacket' Peter used during his stint in the Air Force, Liz finds several key-rings hanging on the same peg. Spreading the key-rings across the kitchen counter, she finds the one which holds the keys that will unlock the office door. There are two keys on the brass ring, a large tubular shaped key and a small tubular shaped key, each has five facets down its tubular length.

Taking the keys back to the office door, Liz pushes the large key into the door lock and turns it until she hears five clicks. At that time, the office door swings open without assistance. Jumping aside, Liz waits until the door has stopped before she steps into the room. Then she walks to the large mahogany desk in the center of the room and pulls the high backed black leather swivel chair out from the desk. However, before she sits, she turns back to shut the door and lock it knowing Peter would have done so.

Then she scolds herself, "Hell, I was married to the guy for thirty years and now he's spooking me to lock his damn door. This isn't the first time I've ever been in here nor will it be the last. After all, Peter has locked his door against real or imaginary people who might sneak into our home, not me."

Liz eases herself into the large chair and takes a deep breath. "Okay, kiddo, let's see what Peter had that he didn't want anyone to see." Though she says the words in jest, they seem to hang in the room. When she turns to the desk, she feels an instant connection to Peter and is comforted by the feeling.

With the door shut, the silence in the room is total and she quickly opens the middle drawer in the desk. Inside, Peter's laptop computer lays in the center of the drawer with a logbook calendar on top. To the right of these is a cell phone wrapped with a leather neck strap which has a badge attached to its clip. The front of the badge shows Peter's face with a thumb-print next to it. Liz reads, "Peter Day, WCA." Turning the badge over, she sees narrow strips of colors through a photo of his eye. There is nothing more to tell her why he had it or why he left it. Deciding it was from one of his many conferences, she drops it back where it had been and closes the drawer.

Turning to the right, she opens the top drawer on that side of the desk and sees it holds office supplies. Closing it again, she pulls open the deep drawer under that and finds personal files for: taxes, investments, general information, and a thick manila envelope labeled: COPIES OF WILLS. Those words take Liz back to the day they'd gone with Bob Drake to their lawyer's office and signed the wills and Bob had signed as witness. It was Bob who she called on June first after the Deputy told her of Peter's plane crash as Bob was not only Peter's business partner, but he was their longtime friend and the executor of their Wills. After Peter's death, Bob had followed Peter's wishes, cleared all debts, notified those needing to be informed and sent death certificates where needed. Since then, Bob had finalized the sale of the company and reinvested her share of the money so her future finances were secure.

Sliding the drawer shut, Liz turns to the left side of the desk and sees there is only one deep drawer on that side. Giving the handle a tug, she is surprised when the drawer doesn't move. Pushing back the chair, Liz crouches in front the drawer and, from that angle, sees a small key hole below the handle which she hadn't seen from the chair. Taking the key ring off the desk, she puts the small key into the equally small keyhole and turns the key as she had for the door lock. However, when there are five clicks, nothing happens and she continues turning the key until there ten clicks from within the lock. At that time, there is a soft buzzing sound and the deep drawer slides out unassisted.

"Well, I'll be damned. Peter Day. What the hell are you hiding in there?" Liz stares at the drawer's contents and is deeply puzzled. At the front of the deep drawer are ten thick manila envelopes standing upright. Lifting one out, she sets it on the desk top. After these envelopes, there are two metal file boxes, one on top of the other. As they fill up the rest of the drawer, she lifts the top one and places it on desk directly in front of her. When she tries to lift the second box, she finds it is much heavier than the first, so she leaves it in the drawer. As she studies the two ominous items in front of her, Liz lifts the manila envelope and turns it around in her hands trying to decide what could be inside. Suddenly afraid of what she will find, Liz drops it back where she'd found it.

Pulling the metal box closer to her, she tries to open the lid and finds it locked. "Hell, I don't need a key for this. A flat-headed screwdriver hit by a good hammer should break open that lock."

Hurrying into the kitchen, she grabs a small tool kit from under the sink and takes it back to the office. Before she goes to the desk, she shuts the door, locks it and smiles as she picks the screwdriver and hammer out of the kit. Peter had laughed when she'd asked for the kit their first Christmas together. However, Liz can't count the number of times she has used one or more of its tools over the years and has no doubts on how to open the metal box.

Laying the box on its back, Liz puts the flathead of the screwdriver into the keyhole of the latch and gives the tool a hard whack with the hammer. The blow drives the sharp edge into the keyhole and, with a twist of her hand, the box's lid pops open.

While the contents spill onto the opened lid of the box, Liz stares dumbfounded at the number of passports which slide into view. Quickly making a rough count, she stops at thirty-six and sees that each passport is bundled with an envelope filled with currency. Each bundle is held together by four thick rubber bands, two around each side. Holding the nearest bundle, Liz's hands shake as she forces the bands from around it. Inside the passport, she sees Peter's face with a different name and address and the country for the currency wrapped with the rubber bands.

Rewrapping the bundle, she drops it on the pile and uprights the metal box with a loud thump. A few passports fall from the open lid when she up righted the box. Taking one at a time, she opens the bundles and checks the passports before she tosses it in with the others. Each passport shows Peter's photo with a different name and address with currency from that country. Each passport she checks is up to date and used within the last two years. When the last bundle is inside the box. Liz whispers, "Peter, who were you? Really?"

Frightened by what she's found, Liz pushes the chair away from the desk and stands, staring into the metal box. Tears slip down her cheeks as she shuts the lid and sets the box back into the drawer. Her hands shake uncontrollably and a deep ache twists her stomach into knots. "All those years I lived with you, Peter, and I didn't know who you were. You weren't the Peter Day I thought I knew. There's only one reason to ever have all of those passports and Bob Drake will have the answers."

Staring into the deep drawer, Liz is about to slam it closed, when she realizes the drawer on the left side of the desk seems shorter than the one she'd opened on the right side of the desk. Pulling both bottom drawers our as far as they can go, she sees the left side drawer is a good third shorter than the drawer on the right side. Pushing the right side drawer slowly back into place, she feels the smoothness of the glides and a slight bump when it is shut.

Standing in front of the drawer to her left, Liz closes it shut, then she pulls it out and it stops with a bump upward. Again she closes the drawer completely and takes hold of the drawer's handle with both hands. Pulling hard, using all her strength, the drawer slides out, gives a hard upward bump then continues to glide out until its full length is exposed.

The contents in the back section of this drawer causes Liz to shout, "Peter, Peter, Peter, what have you hidden in here." Inside the deep drawer are neat rows of bundled one hundred dollar bills. Dumbfounded, Liz picks up one of the bundles, snaps off the rubber band and carefully counts the bills into stacks of ten until there are ten stacks of ten of one hundred dollar bills.

Stunned, she rewraps the bills with its rubber band and sets it to one side of the desktop. Pulling a pad of paper and pen from the supply drawer, Liz counts and tallies until all of the bundles are on top of the desk and in neat piles. "One hundred bundles, of one hundred, one hundred dollar bills equals...? What? No, that can't be right."

Putting her pen down, Liz stares at the stacked bundles in front of her, and nods, "Oh yes, it is right, old girl. Ten thousand dollars per bundle times one hundred bundles makes an even one million dollars, if I counted right. Even if I didn't, that's a hell of a lot of money in that drawer." Moving the stacks from one side of the desk to the other, she recounts and sits back in the chair. "It's true, each bundle is ten thousand, times one hundred bundles, equals one million dollars.

"Peter, you darling man, I don't know where you got this money or what you did for it, but it's mine now. I'm going to do just what you told me to do, hide it in plain sight. That way I'll know where it is and no one else will."

Liz claps her hands with glee as she rushes to the pantry, grabs four black plastic bags from the roll on one of the shelves and rushes back to the office. This time she leaves the door open on purpose as she splits the bundles equally to two of the black plastic bags. Then she drops each into a second bag and folds the excess around the contents and carries them from Peter's office to the pantry.

Dropping the two bags on the floor in front of the chest freezer against the pantry's back wall, Liz opens the lid and removes baskets full of frozen foods. "I don't know where or how you got this loot, Peter, but I'm not handing it over to Bob! He's going to have to ask for it. There are lots of things I can use this money for, lots and lots of things."

When the freezer is empty, she lifts the two bundles of bagged money and places each on the bottom of the freezer. After making certain the contents are spread as level as possible, she methodically returns the baskets of frozen foods to cover the black bags. When the baskets are filled and back in place, Liz smiles with satisfaction. No one opening the freezer would notice there are black bags below the baskets of food.

However, two empty freezer baskets sit on the floor waiting for some use. Looking at the shelves above her, Liz quickly fills the baskets with small items, then sets the baskets where those items had been and look as if the baskets were meant for this sort of use.

Slowly closing the freezer lid, Liz looks up and whispers, "I've done it, Peter. I've hidden your money in plain sight. Now let's see if Bob knows anything about it. If he does, he'll ask for it. If not, it's mine to do with as I want. And best of all, its tax free."

When she goes back into the office, the drawer where the money had been is still open with the manila envelopes and metal boxes showing for anyone to see. Chagrined that she hadn't closed it, she slams it shut causing the desk to shake. Taking the keys off the desktop, she opens the middle drawer and drops them next to the laptop computer and closes it.

Leaning back in the large swivel chair, Liz thinks about what she has discovered about Peter and how many trips he'd gone on 'for the company'. Now she realizes knows those trips were for other things and/or for other places she would never know. Her only contact with him during those times had been his cell phone or through his partner, Bob Drake. A deep sadness sweeps through her as she knows there are only a few jobs which require those types of items and the thought frightens her.

As she pushes the chair back to stand, the phone on the desk rings. Liz lets it ring several times before she answers it. Holding the receiver to her ear, she doesn't say a word. Then she hears Bob Drake's voice, "Liz? Stay in the house, Liz. Lock the doors. Speak to no one. Not on the phone. Not otherwise. Not to anyone. Understand?"

"Yes, Bob, I do. Will you tell me the truth about Peter and your 'company'?"

"Much as I can, Liz, much as allowed. I'll be there in an hour."

After she sets the receiver down, Liz spends the next hour at Peter's desk, her mind whirling with questions that she knows will get no answers. As the hour comes to a close and the next is half gone, her patience wears out and she shouts at the room, "Damn you, Peter Day. Damn you, what did you do on those trips all those years?"

At that moment, the doorbell chimes and Liz calls out, "Who's there?" A man's voice replies, "It's Bob Drake, Liz. Let me in."

When she opens the door, Bob Drake walks past her holding a large metal box in each hand and only nods to her. Setting them on Peter's desk, he turns to Liz and wraps his arms around her and kisses her cheek. "Ah, Liz, I'm sorry you found what you did. I was to get it sooner, but before I could get here, I was called elsewhere. You were never have known any of this. Sorry I'm late today. Fog in the mountains. You know how it gets at times."

Liz chokes, "Yes, Bob, I know about fog."

Chagrined, Bob blushes, "Ah Liz, I'm sorry. Understand I'm as much on edge as you. So before we clear out Pete's office, I'd be forever grateful for a mug of java with a double scotch to sweeten it. It's been a rough day and it's going to get a lot rougher."

Liz leads him into the kitchen and silently measures coffee into the espresso machine and pours scotch into two mugs. Looking at him she asks, "Two jiggers for you, right?"

Bob nods. "Peter taught you well, old girl. Hang on to that thought, as you're in for a rather rough ride. You'll be all right soon enough. Just know Peter was true to you, always."

When they both have their mugs of the strong brew, Bob raises his and toasts, "To the oldest and dearest."

Liz touches her mug to his, "To the oldest and dearest."

Bob downs the hot drink in a few gulps, smacks his lips and sighs. "Liz, you do know how to reach a man's heart. Could you manage another, for each of us, to nurse as we pack up Pete's office?"

"For you, sure. I'll stick to this one, though." She makes the drink and hands it to him. "Here's your crutch, Bob. Let's sit at the table for a bit and tell me what I never knew about Peter. I want answers. No more lies. Yes or no, you and Peter are agents for our government?"

Bob silently follows Liz into the office and sits in the black chair. Across from him, Liz sits in the only other chair and demands to know what they really did. Sipping from his mug for several minutes, Bob sighs and begins, "Peter and I worked for the 'Company'. That is an agency which works for the good of the free world. There was never a business nor a merger nor a sale. The funds you received are legit: from his retirement fund, his life insurance payback, and several large bonuses for work well done. Your stocks and securities are solid as well as your financial status. Most important to you, Liz, is that Peter's love for you was real. You were his one stable thing and he treasured you. We both did."

Liz's blinks back the tears, then says, "Thank you, Bob. I needed to know that I was the only one Peter loved".

"That's all I can say about what Peter did for the Company."

"What? You came all this way, to tell me so little?"

"I told you a whole lot, Liz. You weren't to know any of this, for your own safety. Peter trusted you, know that. You found his office locked this time because of an enemy agent's close proximity in the area. I'm speaking of Alexandria Petrow. Pete worried how much information she got from you. Keep your friends close and your enemies closer. That's why he kept you innocent about Alex and why he traveled less often these last years. More important, he didn't want Alex to view you as a threat to her or those who hired her. Peter's love was solid, Liz. I envied you both. Why do you think I came to visit so often? You are my one stable thing, too, Liz."

Bob's confession passes Liz without notice and she asks, "This spy job was why he died, wasn't it? Peter wouldn't have crashed, not by any mistake he made. He was too good a pilot for that to have happened and he'd bought that exact plane because it glided, for long distances, without power. Somebody did bad things to him. Am I right?"

"The FAA found evidence that shows one bullet entered from the lower right side of the engine compartment, cut the fuel line, then jammed in one valve. He never knew it happened until it was too late and the plane was too low to glide up out of the mountains. The Company's tracking a suspect as we speak."

"Alexandria Petrow?" Liz asks. "She left without a word last week, right after she came to hear what Peter wanted to tell her. Peter came back to see me. Yes, he did. He came within a beam of light that shone from the ceiling, right above the table. He stood in the center of the dining table along with two other people, a red haired man and a beautiful black woman."

Dumbfounded, Bob stares at Liz, then whispers, "Did you just say that Peter was back in this house, on your dining table, standing within a beam of light? Did you say that, Liz? You're really telling me that Peter was here, in this room, after his death, after his cremation?"

"Yes, Bob, Peter stood right in the center of the table. The light came through the ceiling and shone onto the table's surface. He only came back the one night. At first, he took me back through our life together. Then, he demanded that Alex come over so he could talk to her. After she came, it took a while for her to see him, but when she did see him, Peter took over my body and told her what she was to know. I don't know what he said to her as I didn't hear their conversation. After he brought me back, he told me to tell her to choose whether to live or to die. 'If she leaves, she'll live. If she stays, she'll die.' I was shocked by his words and he told me she was an enemy and not to be trusted. Alex heard him say that and ran for the door. However, before she left, she saw the two people with him. Ask her yourself, Bob. That night Alex fled from Redcliff's Beach and hasn't returned. That is the last time I've seen either of them."

Relieved that she's finally able to tell someone about seeing Peter within the light beam, Liz chatters on about the two women now within her home. "Peter brought two women that look exactly as I do. He said they're Parallel Lives of the original Elizabeth Ann Anderson. I see the women at the adjoined dining tables, where the translucent agate is in the floor."

As he listens to Liz, Bob's eyes set into a piercing stare and his jaw tightens. When he's finally able to react, he doesn't speak but stands and turns away, slipping his jacket off his shoulders, he hangs it over the back of the office chair. Then, without a word or glance at Liz, he takes off the shoulder holster with its pistol and lays it on the desk. Finally, he opens both metal boxes he'd brought and sits in the black leather swivel chair and pulls himself up to the desk.

Because of his silence, Liz knows she has told him too much and she stands beside the desk watching him take items from the deep drawer. Neither says a word. Finally, he leans back in the chair, looks directly into Liz's eyes and slaps the desktop. The sharp whack causes Liz to jump backwards hitting the wall behind her.

"Damn it to hell, Liz, what you said is crazy. Don't tell anyone else what you just told me. It's unbelievable to claim Peter came back here. Hell, Liz, Peter died and was cremated. As for Alex telling the truth about anything, haven't you figured out by now that bitch told you anything you wanted to hear? Hell, Liz, it was Alex who ordered Peter's death.

"Yeah! Alexandria Petrow is an enemy agent and she ordered Peter's death. She is, was and always will be, your enemy, Peter's enemy, our country's enemy. Peter let you keep close to her to keep you safe. She would say all sorts of bullshit to you and know you'd tell Peter. We got smart early on and learned to do the exact opposite from what she'd said. That's the only reason her efforts stalled for many years. Hell, Liz, Alex used you to get whatever information you might let slip. Your obsession with her drove Peter crazy. Your Alexandria Peltrow talked true bullshit and you were her best shit spreader."

Bob stares at Liz's shocked face, then slaps the desktop again, "Oh, hell, Liz. You didn't tell her I was coming here today, did you? Not today? Dear God. Please! Say you didn't!"

Liz's face turns red with anger and she glowers at him. "No, Bob, I did not tell anyone. If you'd been listening, instead of judging me, I said earlier that Alex fled Redcliff's Beach right after she saw Peter. That was June fifth. She hasn't returned nor contacted me. Now you understand this, Bob Drake, you will never again tell me I am crazy. Never again. DO YOU UNDERSTAND? I see two others at the adjoined tables. I believe these women exist, though, I don't know how they came to me. I don't care how, I just know they do and they are here to be with me."

Standing, Bob walks around the desk and puts his hands on Liz's shoulders, "Okay, Liz, you've gone through some rough times these past weeks. But, damn it gal, try to get a grip on things. Your mind's slipped a notch and you're seeing things. Real people don't come back after they die. That only happens in films. We need to get you into some counseling."

Shoving him away from her, Liz opens her mouth to shout in anger. However, when she sees the shocked look on his face, it strikes her funny and she begins to laugh. At that moment, Bob reaches for her and Liz slaps his face hard then pushes past him, shouting, "Never touch me again, you bastard. I'm not crazy or mad. I laughed at you, asshole, because you looked such a righteous prig. What a judgmental jerk you are, Bob. Never again talk to me about going to one of your damned doctors. Hell man, I'm the sanest person you'll ever know.

"I'm not the one who's led false lives. I've never had more than one passport or needed more to do espionage. Your people are the ones who need help. Poor Peter, I wish I'd known the burden he carried all those years. Now get those boxes off that desk and get out of my house. Anything you can carry, take tonight. Any furniture, you get out by the end of the week. I want you and Peter's crap out of my life forever. Pack it up and move it out, big boy. I won't tolerate your sneers one more second then necessary."

Without a word, Bob turns to drop Peter's keys into the last metal box and shuts the lid. Taking the boxes to the front door, he sets them down and returns to get his holster off the desktop, slips it over his shoulder then shrugs into his jacket. Going to the front door, he pauses beside Liz and says, "You can stop being angry at me or Peter, Liz. We did what we thought was best. Peter loved you. If I could, I'd like to hear more of the two women. However, I've got to get these boxes back to Seattle, ASAP. As his partner, I'm responsible for their safe delivery. Know that I am always be your good friend and admirer, Liz. One more thing, leave the office door open. Don't shut it. You may need a safe room, if or when Alex returns."

When Liz doesn't respond, Bob returns to the office door and pushes it wide open. Then he checks the lock to make certain it'll open if she closes it accidentally. At that moment, she hears a hissing noise coming from the door jamb. "Noise filters," he says without looking at her. "They're turned off now. The Company's taken control until the equipment's removed."

"That's how you knew to call me last night, isn't it?"

"Yeah, satellite connections are worldwide. When you unlocked the door, the Company knew the office was breached as you didn't punch in the code. That alerted the system and a light flashed on a board, in some hole in the ground somewhere in the world, and sent a message to wherever I was. Headquarters isn't sure what to do about your knowing what you do. We'll let you know later."

When he says the last bit, Liz's head snaps up and she asks, "Are you telling me, I may be eliminated? Do I know too much or is it because

I had an enemy agent as a friend? Are you going to kill me before you leave, Bob? If so, do it quickly."

"What? Good God, no, Liz." Bob shakes his head trying not to laugh. "No, Liz, you're not to be eliminated. I am going to draft you to assist in capturing, Alex when she gets back. We know she traveled to California and did the psychic fairs up the coast. After that, she contacted overseas connections about Peter's death and that you were a spy. Evidently, the fact that you refused her help to clear out Peter's things gave you away. She is also certain you two were never married. She said never believed anyone could be so naïve."

"Naïve? You mean stupid, don't you? Well, I'd say that wasn't my fault, Bob. I knew nothing to tell her. Still don't. Other than what you've just said and from what I saw in that desk drawer. Will she try to kill me? Bob? Answer me. What am I to do? I don't play with guns or have dirty secrets. That's your game, Bob. You have to protect me."

"That's why I'm here, Liz. Getting Peter's things is a ploy to get in without anyone suspecting. There's no real importance to these things. They are as dead as Peter is. We know everything that's in them. However, you should know there is a man in her house, right now, waiting for her to return. He slipped in the night she drove off and is someone we've watched for several years. It's the same guy she claimed to be her brother. Remember? Her only family left in Russia?"

Watching her stare at him, he asks, "Are you going to be alright? I can't stay any longer as Peter's stuff has to be recorded and disposed of tonight. I'll call when we know Alex is on her way home." Seeing Liz's nod, Bob bends to pick up the metal boxes, then stops to look at her.

Instantly, Liz thinks of the money hidden in her freezer and asks, "Are you sure you have everything you need from the office and are you certain you don't want me to close the office door?"

"Yes, to getting all the info and, no, to closing that door. Keep it open. You may need a safe room. If anyone comes snooping around, whether you know them or not, get in that room, close it and turn the three bolts twice. Stay inside until I get there. Understand? Even if Alex seems like her old friendly self. Get in there, slam it closed and lock up. Then, hit the red button on the desk phone. It'll dial us and we'll come."

Before he opens the front door, Bob leans towards Liz and kisses her on the cheek. When she opens her mouth to protest, he stops her with these words, "Things will move fast, Liz. Expect Alex back by the end of the week, no later. When she calls or you see her on the beach, tell her to do this..."

NINE

June 10—Beth

BETH is startled when the first huge wave hits her cabin. Dazed, she tries to understand what she'd been dreaming to cause such a reaction. When a second wave hits the cabin, she cringes under the covers and listens to the winds scream around the south corner of her bedroom. It is the third wave, which sends logs crashing through the north windows, that propels Beth out of bed and into her warmest clothes and boots. Rushing into the hall, she sees a small floater log rolling across the living room floor and one large long one shooting though the shattered north window. Shredded shutters flap dangerously as strong gusts beat them against the outer wall and through shattered window panes. While she watches, a wave crashes over the deck sending another log through the glass slider door. The log rolls across the room, slams into the kitchen counter and bullets back to shatter the rest of the glass on the beach side of the cabin.

Flinging open the hall closet door, Beth pulls on her heaviest jacket, hangs her purse off one shoulder and grabs the two metal boxes containing personal and financial information before she pushes open the front door and goes into the carport where the pickup sits. Tossing everything onto the pickup's passenger seat, she rushes to the other side and jumps behind the steering wheel. Finding the trucks key in the ignition where she always leaves it, she starts the engine and backs the vehicle up the driveway, then parks it on the shoulder of Shoreline Drive. From there, she sees how hard the storm is battering her cabin and, for several minutes, tries to decide whether to flee or stay to watch the cabin's destruction.

Lightening zigzags across the sky showing her the devastation on the beach with every flash. To the north, the last few of the sand dunes are sucked away with each crashing wave. Pounding on the steering wheel, Beth shouts, "This one is bad, Max. This is it. The cabin will go this time. It's going to be washed away like those others forty years ago. Maxine? Oh, Max, Max, I forgot us. I forgot the photos of our life together. Maxine, I can't lose you again… never again."

Pushing open the truck door, she struggles against the strong wind as she staggers down the driveway and into the carport. Once she's through the front door, Beth yanks a large wheeled duffle bag from the hall closet, then stuffs the framed photos off walls and her photo albums into the bag. When the duffle bag is jammed full, she wrestles it to the front door. However, as she rolls it off the jamb to the first step into the garage, the heavy bag jerks out of her hands at the same time a strong wind gust blows through the cabin. Stumbling forward, Beth overcorrects herself backwards and smacks the side of her head on the doorjamb.

Dazed, Beth pulls the heavy bag up the driveway and, with the strong wind at her back, reaches the truck. However, the same harsh wind holds the pickup door firmly shut no matter how hard Beth tugs at its handle. When there is a sudden lull in the wind, she is able to yank the door open and she pushes the duffle bag onto the passenger seat. As soon she slams that door, she scrambles around to the other side of the pickup and falls onto the driver's seat. Again, Beth tries to decide whether to stay or leave. However, the decision is made for her as the blow to her head takes over and she passes out against the steering wheel.

Several hours later, Beth is awakened by the sun shining on her face and, when she tries to sit up, her head pounds with a sharp pain. Puzzled as to where she is or why her head hurts so hard, she touches it along the left side and feels a large bump. "What the hell happened? I'm inside my truck yet my head feels like it's been split in two. Damn it hurts, damn, damn, damn."

Struggling into a more upright position, she leans her head back against the seat and turns it slowly to the right. To her surprise and relief, the cabin still stands. However, the driveway seems heaped with debris and logs of many sizes. Several long thick logs lay crisscrossed over and around shorter logs and piles of debris. The sight jogs her memory and Beth slowly remembers the events of the night before: the waves, the wind, the truck, the photos, and even the hard blow when her head hit against the doorjamb.

"Maxine, I hate to say this, but I don't think I could have saved you. If you'd still been in the hospital bed, I don't think I could have saved you, my darling. It's almost a blessing that you died when you did, long before this horrible storm tore through our cabin. I don't know if the cabin can be saved or even if it's strong enough for me to walk through. I'm going to try. Thank God, I saved our photos, Max. I saved our memories of our time together, you and me, forever." Shattered by the intense reality of the storm's aftermath, Beth lays her head on the steering wheel and sobs. Then, as if Maxine were shouting at her, Beth hears, *Stop that sniveling and go get help.*

Chagrinned, Beth sits up and looks around expecting someone to be next to the truck or in it with her. Seeing there is no one, she opens the truck door and gingerly steps onto the road. Straining against the wind, she sees that several huge logs now lay over the driveway blocking her way to the carport. Without stopping, she reaches across the top of the first hug log, pulls herself up and lays on her stomach. Swinging her legs over to the other side, she lets herself slide to the ground and repeats the moves over the next several logs until she reaches the carport. The inside of this space is piled with debris and Beth walks around them to reach the steps to the front door of her cabin. Using her feet to sweep a mess from both steps, she is soon able to open the door and go inside.

Talking a deep breath, she turns the doorknob and steps into the short hallway by the guest room. Instantly, she sees the doors to both bedrooms and the bath are shut. When she opens the bathroom door, she finds the room untouched except for a skiff of wet sand across the tiled floor. Relief floods through Beth and she quickly opens the door to the guestroom and stands looking at the room's interior for several seconds, before she laughs out loud, "Holy cow...The stones in Dad's fireplace wall must have deflected the float logs up to the driveway. There's not even a crack in the widows and the room is clean and dry. Even the shutter over the window is intact."

Turning back to the cabin's main room, she sees a completely different picture. Piles of flotsam, logs and shattered glass are everywhere. Each window along with the slider door has been shattered. Only a few splinters, from the heavy shutters, show something had once protected the windows. Logs of many lengths and sizes lie across the area where the hospital bed had sat only two weeks before. Everywhere she looks there are logs piled upon logs. Many stick through or out empty window frames. A bookcase lies smashed against the kitchen counter with the books mixed amongst piles of flotsam and shattered glass.

However, when she sees the long dining table sitting untouched in front of the stone fireplace and the translucent golden stone in the floor still glowing under the piles of logs and debris, Beth sighs and say, "Thank you Daddy. Thank you."

Immediately she sees there is no way to reach the kitchen as it is filled with piles of debris. The mess has buried the counter tops until it spills out the shattered south window. However, the upper cabinet doors are shut tight and Beth crawls along a large log to where the end of the lower cabinet under the end of the counter. Pulling debris away, she is able to crack its door enough to see the contents are clean and dry.

Bursting into tears, she cries out, "Daddy, Daddy, you kitchen held. It held against the storm. Thank you, thank you, darling Daddy, for expecting the worst and building our cabin to hold against it."

Finally, she walks to her bedroom door and opening it, Beth shrieks with disbelief, "It's as I left it! The wind must have slammed the door shut right after I left. There's a bit of sand here and there, but not much. The south window just cracked but didn't blow out. My God, Max, this is an easy fix. If our cabin can survive this storm, so can I. But, what to do first? Who'll bring me the help I need. Yes, George Ames, Finally I'll get some use from all that insurance I've carried for years. Where's his the number? George will know what I'm to do. Maxine, thanks for insisting I pay those years of premiums?"

As the house phone still sits on the nightstand beside the bed, Beth lifts the receiver and hears a dial tone. Thumbing through the index file setting next to it, she finds the George Ames Insurance Agency phone number and dials. When the man answers, Beth fills him in on what happened and Ames tells her not to move a thing, but to make a list of what she sees and knows is missing. He'll be there within the hour. Hanging up the receiver, she whispers, "Maxine, I know you're the angel that rode on my shoulder last night and now I've found an earth angel named George Ames. He's sending people to clean up the mess and make the cabin right again. Maybe the cabin and I'll both survive. With you and George on my side, maybe this will be an easy do-over."

Taking a notepad from the nightstand's drawer, Beth goes into the main room and begins to list what she sees is missing or damaged. After she has done the inside, she goes out to see what damage has been done there and around the outside of the cabin. When finished, she is walks into the carport and hears a horn honk. Turning she sees a large SUV parking at the top of the driveway. The man inside honks and waves as he opens the door to climb out. Waving back, Beth walks to the large log outside the carport and Ames shouts for her to stay there. Walking down the south slope of the driveway, he edges around the end of the logs and debris. When he reaches the carport, he tells her, "I'm amazed your cabin is still standing. The beach south of here is piled high with debris, all the way down to the south cliffs. Further south, the beaches got lucky as the storm turned back out to sea. Ocean Shores was missed completely. Let me see that list you've started and let's walk the house together. You ready?"

As Beth hands over the writing pad, she notices her hand is shaking and Ames tells her, "I want you to stop right now and take five big breathes. That's good. Now, have you had any water this morning? No? Do you have any bottled water out here or in the house?" When she points to the built-in cabinets along the south wall of the garage, Ames clears debris away from the cabinet and opens its door. Three large boxes of bottled water seem to shout at her and she gratefully takes the one George Ames hands her. Taking one out for himself, they both drink their fill before George leads her into the cabin.

When she shows him the three rooms that stayed clean, Ames declares them a miracle. However, when he has to stop next to the table in front of the fireplace, he stares silently at the room and begins to ask Beth questions. Then, he writes notes on each of her replies and adds items to the list which she hadn't thought were damaged. When she questions him, Ames explains, "We've learned to replace all electrical appliances as salt water corrodes wiring and sand is impossible to get out. The cabin will have to be rewired. Don't use any lights or electrical equipment. We don't want fire damage added to this list. The cleanup crew comes with their own generators."

When he points out at the deck, he says, "Let's check outside for damage there. The deck looks badly broken on the south end." Beth follows him without comment and they walk the perimeter of the cabin. When they're back inside the carport, Ames asks, "Want to hear the good news first?" When Beth nods, he laughs, "Good. I like to start with the good and you've got a lot of good to hear about. Here's what I think that can be done. Those logs filling the driveway and cabin are almost a blessing as they can be used to rebuild the decks and build frontage around the west and north sides of the cabin. That's a great bonus, as that sort of timber is very expensive. If done right these logs will protect the cabin from many more years of storms.

"You already know your father did a great job on the original cabin as he anchored steel rods into bedrock and bolted everything to that pad of concrete. Those two things and the six by six trusses and uprights are what held the cabin together and the copper roof has hardly a scratch. As you already found out, the kitchen cabinets are in great shape and will be good as new with minimal effort on your part after the cleaning crew gets the cabin cleaned out.

"The first thing will be to clear the driveway and then work through the cabin. The cleanup crew is on the way up with dumpster trucks and will clean off the drive and the cabin. Then they'll give the whole place a good hosing down, inside and out. They've a water-tank truck for that. The three rooms, bedrooms and bath, will be left for you to do. Expect all the appliances, big and small, to be gone by the end of the day. The leather furniture and table were saved by the massive stones in the fireplace. "As I said, saltwater and sand ruin electrical wiring, so an electrician will be out in two or three days to rewire the cabin. He needs things to dry out a bit before he can rewire and hook you back into the grid.

"My brother, Tom Ames, has a heavy equipment business that builds bulkheads and decks. He works throughout the Northwest and is between jobs right now and will be here before eight this morning, about the same as the cleanup crew. Stay close to the cabin till both get here as you need to sign work orders as nothing'll get started till you do. My next instruction is easy, though sometimes it's the hardest to do. Don't worry. That's the bad I told you about. The worry. Don't do it. I expect your home will be better than new by week's end. What you must do, once you've signed the work orders, is get out of here and stay out of the crews' way. Go walk the beach to the south. Find your things. The next high tide isn't till five. Don't let what's worth saving be swept out to sea. You'll be surprised by what you'll find. Anything that can be restored and reused is money in your pocket. Search the beach, thoroughly, down to the south cliffs."

As Ames talks, Beth walks him out to his rig. At that time, he points at her pickup and says, "Move your pick-up further north. The crews' trucks need lots of room to maneuver and Tom will want to park his equipment trailer as close to the cabin as possible."

After Ames drives away, Beth drives her truck to the roundabout at the end of Shoreline Drive and comes back a half mile before she parks it on the shoulder of the road. When she reaches the north side of her property, she studies the damage to the cabin and the logs poking out the north windows and hanging off the deck. Stunned by the scene, she whispers, "You know, God, when I asked for something to get me through the days after Max's death, I didn't mean for you to send one of your perfect storms. I do thank you for not sending it while Maxine still lived as I wouldn't have been able to save either of us."

In less than an hour, Beth hears the sounds of big trucks rounding the south curve and heading up Shoreline Drive. Then two dump trucks, a double tank truck and two vans, filled with the work crew and pulling huge dumpsters, stop at the top of her drive. When the vehicles' doors open, eight hefty men and women unload and one man stomps around and over the debris to greet Beth. He introduces himself as the 'Super' of the cleanup crew and hands her a work order to sign. After she does, he takes it to the van and the crew starts cleaning off the top of the driveway.

Suddenly aware that she must get out of the way, Beth hurries into the carport and lifts the old beach wagon off its hook on the west wall and carries it over to the south side of the driveway. Then she pulls a pack from the storage cabinet and fills it with bottled water and two boxes of energy bars and sets the pack into the long wagon. Pulling it down the slope of the sand dune to the beach below, she parks it below the deck barely clinging to the south corner of the cabin. From that angle, she realizes the deck had broken loose and tilts dangerously low to the sand.

While she's wondering how it will ever be repaired, the sound of heavy equipment comes from the south curve on Shoreline Drive and she hurries back to the front of the carport. A large dump truck pulling an equipment trailer loaded with a large massive digger/dozer slows as it passes the driveway and the driver yells he's going to turn around and park close to the cabin as possible. Guessing the man must be Tom Ames, Beth waves. However, not one of the cleanup crew stop or acknowledge the trucks passing and keep shoveling debris from the driveway into the closest dumpster.

By the time, Ames parks his rig, Beth has worked her way along the north side of the driveway and greets him as he steps out of his truck. "Hi, Tom, I'm Beth Anderson. George told me you'd be coming up so I moved my pickup earlier to give you room to park your equipment close to the cabin. I sure thank you for getting here so fast. The clean-up crew got here fifteen minutes ago and I signed their work order. I understand you also have one I need to sign, don't you?"

When Beth finishes, she takes a deep breath and Tom Ames erupts with laughter. "My God gal, I thought you were never going to take a breath. Your adrenalin must be pumping overtime. To answer you, yes, I'm Tom Ames, George's brother, and I'm very pleased to get this work. Now, breathe and sign here. Then, let's go see what needs to be done."

Laughing with him, Beth signs the paper and they go down to where the cleanup crew is working. When Tom reaches the Super, the crew stops working and waits as the two men talk. Then, as Tom walks back to his equipment, the Super tells his crew what to expect Tom to do. Beth is amazed at how fast the huge digger/dozer is unloaded off the trailer and moves to the first huge float log blocking the driveway. Everyone in the crew walks back to Shoreline Drive and the cab on the dozer swings around so that the claw on the equipment reaches forward until it is over the massive log. At that point, Ames steps off to study the log's size and talk with the cleanup crew.

After he explains how and where he'll move each log from the driveway and then from the cabin, he says, "All these will be used around the cabin or on the beach. After I've got those out of the crew's way, they can move the small logs off to the north side and let them roll down to where I've moved the large ones. Then, I'll lift the one from the cabin's windows. After that I'll be working on and around the deck.

"I'll try to keep ahead of your work and if you come to anything too heavy to carry, give me a shout. We'll team up to pull it out somehow. You can toss small logs out the north windows or place one end on a window frame. I'll pluck it from there. Once I clear the drive, you can roll your dumpsters down and shovel directly to them. We should have this mess cleared by afternoon."

Turning to Beth, he frowns menacingly as he says, "You... get the hell out of here. Go search the south beach for your things. Stay away from both cabin and driveway. Nobody wants you crushed by a truck, dozer, or rolling logs. Don't come back till after five to sign off on the work orders."

So relieved to have someone else do what she sees as an impossible job, Beth simply nods and walks into the cabin to make certain the bedroom and bathroom doors are shut tight. When she returns to the carport, Ames' digger/dozer is lifting a huge log and swinging it off the north side of the drive. Scrambling back inside the cabin, Beth slips over logs and piles of debris to get out to the deck. Sliding down to the railing on the sloping deck, she holds on until she sees the wagon and pack below. Then she measures where her own landing should be and takes a deep breath, counts to three and leaps off to the sand, ten feet below. Landing squarely on both feet, she bounces once and breathes a sigh of relief. Picking up the wagon's handle, she begins her hike down the south beach, pulling the wagon behind her.

As she scours the beach, she's halfway to the south cliffs, before Beth stops for a break. Opening a bottle of water, she drinks and studies the long line of items she'd placed in the dry sand above the outgoing tide. Amazed at what items found that could be cleaned and reused, Beth feels as if things are starting to go her way. When her stomach growls loudly, she unwraps and eats two energy bars then, finishes the bottle of water. Returning the trash to the backpack, she returns to her search for things washed onto the beach.

Soon, the strip of high dry sand is strung with all sorts of items: books, lamps with shades or no shades, two of the six dining chairs, the large wooden deck table she'd chained to the corner of the now sloping deck, two area rugs from the living area, an end-table hardly scratched and one with a missing a leg. Best of all, she finds Maxine's bentwood rocker wrapped in a pile of flotsam with hardly a scratch on it.

When she reaches the south cliffs, the sun is high in the sky and her body feels the five mile trek. Sitting on the wagon, she drinks from another bottle of water and eats two more energy bars. Looking north, Beth notices how her cabin seems to hover above the beach. Knowing this is an illusions caused by the wavering heat waves reflected off the sand, she enjoys the shimmering effect the work crew's movements make. For several minutes, she watches as if spellbound. The moment is broken by a flight of sandpipers whipping onto the exposed tide flat in front of her. As she watches their progress up the beach, she whispers, "Maybe, just maybe, the cabin will last another year or two. I sure hope so."

Stuffing the bottle and wrappers into the pack, she stretches and bends to get the kinks from her body. Then she realizes she needs a potty break and goes to the cliff and squats behind the larger boulders at its base. When Beth is zipping up her jeans, a shower of pebbles spatter over her shoulders causing her to glance back in time to see something large moving off the cliff face, Leaping from behind the boulders, she races to the edge of the waves without looking back. As she runs, she hears a loud thudding sound and the ground vibrates under her feet. Dumbfounded, she whirls around and sees that a massive hunk has fallen off the granite cliff face and shattered over the boulders she'd squatted behind only seconds before.

Instantly, Beth runs to pull the beach wagon away from the falling rocks bouncing onto the slab then flying in every direction. When the dust finally settles, Beth studies the cliff face and sees exactly where the huge slab had been attached and is shaken by how close she'd come to being crushed under the massive stone.

As she stares at the newly exposed cliff face, something catches her eye and she realizes there is a large translucent stone bulging outward from the surface of the cliff. The large rounded agate's shape looks to be the size and color of her touchstone set in the north cliffs. The beautiful stone glows brightly in the sunlight and Beth moves cautiously around the edge of the granite slab looking for a place low enough to climb onto its surface.

Finally she finds two short logs and jams them next to the cliff face to create a pair of sturdy steps. Using these, she climbs onto the stone slab's surface and cautiously crosses to stand in front of the newly exposed translucent agate. Putting both hands on its protruding surface, she feels a strong vibration and jerks them away again. Staring at the glowing stone, she touches it with only her fingertips. Instantly, her hands are pulled to the stone's surface and held there by some unseen force. Again, the stone hums under her hands. However, this time, she finds the vibration comforting and she rubs her hands over the stone's smooth surface.

At this close examination, she sees the glowing effect comes from within the core of the stone and looks very much like the stone in the floor of her cabin. Trying to pull away, her hands are held to the stone's surface and Beth slides her hands across the large protruding melon sized surface trying to find a way to break the connection to the stone. As she moves her hands from one area of the stone to another, she pushes and pulls against the bulging shape yet her hands are held tight to its surface.

Finally exhausted, Beth stops moving and rests her head against the bulge of the stone. After a few minutes, she steps back as far as she's able to and rotates her hands out along the edges where the stone is attached to the cliff face. Suddenly, as if planned, the entire protruding exterior of the translucent stone comes away in her hands as if glued to them. Startled by the stone's sudden release from the cliff face, Beth realizes she is unable to let go of it and is puzzled about what to do next. At first, the weight of the large stone doesn't bother her, but after she's held it for a few minutes the weight becomes almost unbearable.

Frightened, she stumbles off the granite slab and staggers to the beach wagon as there seems to be no way to set the stone down without damaging it or herself. Kneeling in the soft sand, she places the rounded hunk into the back of the wagon and flops onto the sand beside it. Exhausted, by the effort and her emotions, she lays beside the wagon for several minutes. Turning her head to look at the stone, she sees the golden hunk of translucent agate has the shape of a large glowing bowl.

Sitting up, Beth gently touches the beautiful shape and hears a pure ringing tone as each finger slides across the bowl's rim. Turning the stone around where it sits in the wagon, she sees it is over two feet in width and a good three feet in height. Amazed, she runs her fingertips around the smooth thick shape and hears the same pure notes coming from deep inside the stone bowl.

Suddenly, her mind is full of words that tell her how the storm came to send her out to the south beach to be at the south cliffs at the time the cliff face fell away. Beth hears that she was given the agate bowl to be centered over the stone in the floor of the cabin and that it must be done before sundown. Beth feels these words more than she hears them and everything said to her seems clear and understandable to her. There are no questions as to why these things have happened, only that they were to be done.

Beth understands how one thing led her to the next and then on to the next, until she was where she needed to be to find the glowing stone bowl. As she walks north, she comes to understand why her Dad was drawn to the north cliffs to find the glowing hunk from her touchstone and why he placed the hunk which came off in his hands into the floor of his cabin. Her Dad had always said he'd been told to do it just as he had done it. Now, Beth is told to take the stone bowl to her home and place it on her table directly over the translucent stone in the floor.

Shivers cross her shoulders as this knowledge is revealed to her. "Why me? Why am I to be the keeper of this amazing stone? Whoever brought me to this place, this day, at this moment, please, tell me. What am I to do with this information? Why me?"

Do not question your duty. Take the stone to be with the other in your home. It is your charge to do so, ELIZABETH ANN ANDERSON, for you are the original child of all the Elizabeth Ann's.

Stunned by the words, Beth stops to stare at the agate bowl for several minutes. As she does, she scoops sand into the wagon bed to hold the bowl so it will not tip over. Once the bowl is secured by the sand, Beth turns to look back at the cliff face and is stunned by what she sees.

The huge granite slab no longer sits at the base of the cliff face. The area is back to how it looked when she first reached the cliffs at noon. The cliff face is flat and the massive hunk of granite stone is nowhere to be seen. The boulders she'd peed behind are where they'd been and the translucent agate, left after the bowl had come off in her hands, is no longer there. The south cliffs look as they had for as long as Beth can remember. The only evidence, that anything happened at these cliffs today, is the amazing translucent agate bowl in the beach wagon.

Suddenly, Beth feels an urgency to go home and she begins the five mile trek back to the cabin. As she goes, she passes the many things she'd set on the dry sand earlier that day, yet she doesn't stop for now she knows that collecting these things from the beach was not the reason for her to be out there. With this knowledge, Beth accepts the responsibility for the large agate bowl and fills gratitude for the gift of unbelievable beauty.

When her acceptance of duty reaches the Universal Plains, a flash of brilliant light streaks through her dimension and connects the touchstone in the north cliffs, to the agate in the floor of her cabin, to the translucent agate bowl in the wagon and south to the agate within the south cliffs.

Long before she reaches the cabin, Beth can tell the cleanup crew and Tom Ames' heavy equipment are no longer on the beach nor are there any trucks parked along Shoreline Drive. The silence which greets her is a welcomed relief. From the beach below the cabin, she sees how Tom Ames leveled the deck with long float logs and bolted the decking back into place. Looking at the bulkheads around the cabin, she is amazed at the amount of work he'd been able to do in one day.

Slowly pulling the wagon up the slope of sand south of the driveway, she sees Ames' digger/dozer parked off the other side of the drive and the trailer still where it'd been parked by Tom, along Shoreline Drive. However, his truck is gone and she knows that means he will return to finish what still has to be done.

Pulling the wagon into the carport, Beth realizes she sees a miracle. The driveway and carport are cleared and perfectly clean. There is not one thing, on or around the driveway, to show what a horrible mess the storm had left the night before. The driveway's surface has been swept and hosed clean. Even the shoulders along the driveway have been raked clean.

Pulling the wagon to the front steps, she steps up to the door and opens it. Tears spring into her eyes as she cries out, "I never thought the cabin would look this good ever again. What a great job those people did here. I must call George Ames to thank him for sending me those angels. Tom Ames, too."

Walking through the rooms, she finds the signed work orders on the kitchen counter with a note from Tom Ames saying he'd done the walk through with the crew's Super and, if anything was missed, give him a call, otherwise, he'll see her at six tomorrow morning. Checking the rest of the cabin, Beth is amazed that the devastating mess of that morning is gone.

Even the leather sofa and matching chairs have been scrubbed and grouped in front of the fireplace. Once more, the long dining table sits directly over the translucent agate in the gleaming concrete floor and Beth is amazed that there is little damage to it. As she walks around it, she runs her hand along the edges and whispers, "How the hell did you hide from all those logs, old girl? You're a sure sign that this whole thing was a miracle."

Stepping back from the table, she sees the agate in the floor is glowing brighter than she's ever seen it before. "Of course, you know the bowl is close to you. I'll go get." Rushing out to the carport, she carefully lifts the large agate bowl from the wagon. Tilting it to one side, she pours the sand from the inside and wipes it clean with an old towel from the corner cabinet. Then, she carries the heavy translucent stone bowl into the cabin and places it on the dining table. Sliding it to the center of the table, she steps away to see the effect.

At once, the agate in the floor becomes brilliant and the agate bowl responds in kind. Soon the two stones pulse with a tantalizing tempo and become so brilliant that Beth must turn away, yet a joyous emotion brings a feeling of happiness she has not felt for over a year and she knows the stones are so precious that she must not leave the cabin until it is totally secured.

Hurrying into her bedroom, she pulls her sleeping bag from the closet shelf and picks the quilt and pillow off her bed. Going back to the main room, she sees the light within each agate has diminished to a soft pulsing glow. Doubling the quilt, she lays it over the damp sofa cushions, then spreads the sleeping bag on top of that and puts the pillow at its open end.

Going into the kitchen, she turns on the cold water tap and sees it runs clear. Taking a glass from the cupboard, she fills it with water and drinks it, finding it pure. Taking a can of ravioli off a pantry shelf, she opens it and eats directly from the can. When finished, she puts the can into the container under the sink and sees the container of bug spray. Taking it over to the sofa, she sprays over the sleeping bag and gives a spritz over her head. Then she puts it back where she found it and when she stands, she looks out the window over the sink.

In the far distance, she sees a bright light winking from the cliff face of the south cliffs, five miles away. Staring at the light, she says, "What the hell do you think you're doing now? That stone slab of granite covered you again. I saw your cliff face had returned to what it'd been before I was given that protruding part of your agate. What's happening? Missing your kid already? Well, the bowl's safely on my table and I'm not giving it back."

When these words pop out of her mouth, Beth realizes the wall around the window has lit and she turns to see the two agates are again glowing brightly. Suddenly irritated with the whole intrusive phenomenon, Beth shouts, "Settle down, you two, settle down, right now, I'm going to bed and I want to sleep. So shut down."

Instantly, both agates dim and surprises Beth so much that she laughs and feels more in control of her life than she has for many months. Without another word, she climbs into her sleeping bag, zips it to her chin, and is asleep within minutes.

Through the night, the stones in her home and the stones in the cliff faces pulse with the same rhythm and share knowledge held for thousands of years. As Beth sleeps, the information is passed on to her.

TEN

June 10—Eliza

ELIZA pours a shot of cream into her mug of coffee and turns off the machine sitting on the kitchen counter in the W's. Walking onto the high lanai, she sinks into her favorite wicker chair to begin her morning. Sighing with relief, she is grateful to be back home after last week's Grand Jury in Hood River. Studying the full six miles of Redcliff's Beach, she tries to ignore memories that rush into her head. However, unable to do so, her head soon whirls with all that happened the past three weeks.

Her cell phone vibrates in the pocket of her robe, she sees it's her sister, Marie calling. Pleased to have the distraction from her thoughts, Eliza answers and a wide smile changes her face and attitude. "Hello, darling. Good morning to you, too. How great you called, I'm in the W's and just sent you a mental thank you, again, for insisting we put Dad's kitchen up here. I'm on the lanai with a mug of delicious coffee from the new brewer. Must say, it's a great way to start my day. The view up here is truly amazing. I'm so high above the beach that barely a sound reaches me. Of course, the gulls aren't too happy I've taken over their perch. You need to move here, ASAP, and enjoy this with me. When is that house of yours going to sell?"

Laughing, Marie answers, "That's why I called, Sis. I have a buyer and the deal is to close this afternoon. If things go as they should, I'll be moved up by July fourth. I've a mover on standby and will bring a load of personal items up next weekend. I wanted to tell you how sorry I was to have to work that job in Portland on the last day of the Grand Jury. Was any decision made by the jury?"

"No, not really. The verdict was the killing was done be persons unknown and the Judge disbanded the Jury as there were no formal charges. My lawyer said that happens more often than most people think. However, let's not talk about that right now. I want to thank you for letting me stay at your place that horrible week. Having you with me was a great help. You made the week enjoyable and I thank you again. Is there anything I can do for you at this end?"

"Not really. As I said, I'll bring a load next weekend and re-measure my rooms. I don't want to haul unnecessary furniture but I sure don't want to dump stuff I love, either. How was your trip home?"

"Traffic was good and I must say it's great to be back. As for things you want here, bring only what's important to you. After you sell the house, you'll have money to buy new stuff which might fit into your new suite and lifestyle. Besides, I'd love shopping with you as you did with me. Now that I've lived here a while, I see where we could use a few more things on the first floor. I'll show you what I mean when you get here. Can't wait for you to see what I did with my rooms. Gosh, Marie, it's going to be so great having you up here fulltime."

After the sisters say their goodbyes, Eliza takes her empty mug to the sink, washes it and sets it in the drainer. Then, she goes down to her suite, on the second floor, and slips into a pair of jeans and a dark purple tee-shirt with 'ALOHA' written across it in hot-pink. Looking at herself in the mirror, Eliza chuckles at the letters marching directly across her ample bosom.

Going to the main floor, she opens the glass sliders and walks out to the railing of the extended beach deck. Looking to the north red cliffs. "It's so good to be home. I never want to leave Redcliff's Beach again. I'm done with the outside world. This is where I belong for as long as I live."

In that instant, her thoughts flash back over her week in Hood River and the Grand Jury that convened about Jack's and Peg's deaths. More now than at the time, Eliza is amazed how her statement meshed with the one her neighbors, Al and Penny, gave. Even more puzzling was how Mike Hartman's alibis fell apart the more he spoke about going to Chili, then of flying to New York City and being with his woman friend. When called to testify, the woman confirmed Mike was with her when the murders happened and the two were together when the news was reported on CNN. She said Mike called Sheriff Frank Gilbert in Hood River and flew home to be at the Grand Jury. Sheriff Gilbert testified he interviewed Mike twice, once over the phone and again when he met Mike at the plane.

After rereading Mike's statements, Gilbert called the woman back to check Mike's story and, at that time, she told him she planned to divorce her husband and marry Mike. It was those words which caused the Grand Jury to demand the woman testify in person. It was also when Mike began to visibly sweat. When she took the stand, the woman admitted Mike had not asked her to marry him, only implied it. However, when Mike was again questioned, he said he loved the woman and would have married her had they both been single. Then, he shouted, "That doesn't mean I'd ever kill Peg. I'd never kill, not anyone. Never."

Thinking over those moments, Eliza realizes the woman's testimony hurt Mike more than it helped him and the trial ended with half the town certain Mike had killed Jack and Peg, while the other half was certain Eliza had something to do with the killing.

When the Judge announced the Jury's decision, 'that the killings were done by person or persons unknown', the room erupted with laughter. Eliza stunned everyone, including herself, when she burst into tears and shocked the crowded room to silence.

I admit it. I loved Jack at the beginning of our marriage and even a bit at the end. He broke my heart in a thousand ways. I regret killing him but not killing Peg. She deserved to die. She betrayed me. Lied to me over and over. All those years, she insisted she hated Jack. His betrayal I got used to years ago. Never will hers. Never.

She was my good friend for years. How could she betray me like that? Mike looked so sad at the trial. I didn't say a word to him. What's to say? His wife killed with her head in Jack's crotch? I doubt words would never ease that fact.

Shaking off the thoughts, Eliza turns to go into her home. However, instead of the wide open deck she'd come out on, the deck now is closer to the house and has low benches around the edges instead of the railing hers does. Puzzled, she tries to understand what she sees. At that moment, a woman with short white hair comes out the open slider door and walks up to Eliza.

Smiling, the woman says, "You're the other Elizabeth Ann Anderson which Beth and I saw the other day, aren't you? Of course, you are. I can tell by your shoulder length hair. Can't you see yourself in my face? I, too, was born Elizabeth Ann Anderson and am now Liz Day."

Instantly, Eliza backs away and asks, "What have you done with my home? What is it you want from me?"

"I only want to get to know you. At least tell me your name. I've told you mine is Liz Day and named Elizabeth Ann Anderson by my parents, James and Jill Anderson. They were both killed in a terrible car accident when I was fourteen, as was my sister, Dana. We lived in Hood River, Oregon, until I was ten. At that time, Dad moved our family to Seattle. Does any of this sound familiar to you?"

Eliza whispers, "I'm not you. I'm Eliza Staples. Born Elizabeth Ann Anderson to my parents in Hood River. Yes, their names were James and Jill Anderson, but my father died when I was ten and Mom and I stayed in Hood River. Now that I've answered your questions, I want you to leave and never bother me again. Too much has happened to me this month. My husband died the first of June first and I haven't gotten over it. I beg you, please, leave me alone."

Liz exclaims, "He died on June first? My husband was killed when his airplane crashed on that date and Beth's partner, Maxine, died that day, too. You said your name is Eliza Staples? Eliza, it's so good to meet you. Thank you for telling me so much. I saw Beth early this morning. She was standing with a man looking at a mess in her cabin. It was filled with logs and debris. Did you see her? She's the one with the ponytailed hair."

Eliza screams, "Didn't you hear me? I don't care about you or that other woman. She tried to push me out of my own doorway. Leave me alone." Then Eliza runs down the steps off the deck to the path through the high sand dunes. She doesn't stop running until she reaches the edge of the waves. Shaking, she turns back at her house and is shocked to see no one on her deck and no one came after her.

Staring at her house for several minutes, Eliza tries to calm herself. Then completely dismayed, she mutters, "Killing Jack has turned my head inside out. Dear God, how will I ever get out of this terror I caused?"

Before going into her home, Eliza peers through the open slider door and sees nothing unusual in the main room of her home. Once inside, she searches through each room on the three floors to make certain no one is hiding there. When she fills a glass with ice and pours a can of soda over it, she sees her hands shake badly. Going outside to sit on a chaise lounge, she lays back in the chaise to let the sunshine calm her nerves.

However, her mind continues to spin over the times she's seen the two women. "How can there be two woman who look exactly like me in every way except my hair length? This must come from guilt or stress. I must remember those women aren't real. And, I've got to stop talking to myself. Good lord, I'm doing it right now. Shit, I'll either hang myself or be hauled off to the loony-bin."

Footsteps on the decking cause Eliza to look where the slider doors of her home should be. Instead, she sees an open slider with shattered glass spread across the deck and the ponytailed woman walks through piles of debris. As she moves past the end of the chaise where Eliza lies, the woman grabs onto the railing of a badly tilted deck and slides down a ways before she lets go and lands on the sand below.

Standing in the corner of the railing, Eliza watches the woman walk to a large wagon parked several feet down the beach. Stunned, Eliza shouts, "You there, stop where you are. What were you doing in my house? Who are you?"

However, the ponytailed woman picks up the wagon's handle and pulls it down the beach without looking behind her. Stunned, Eliza recognizes the wagon as the one from her own childhood, the same one her Dad had built to pull Eliza and Marie on all the family's beach walks to the hollow tree trunk and their family picnics. While Eliza watches, the woman crisscrosses sand dunes on an empty five mile beach towards the south cliffs and pulls items out of the sand and places them above the tide line on dry sand.

There is no one else on the flat narrow beach nor are there any other structures. There is only this cabin and flocks of seabirds. The only person is the lone woman, her ponytailed hair swishing behind her head, as she pokes through debris piles.

Eliza exclaims, "Flat empty beach? How can that be? Where are the sea grass topped sand dunes of my beach? How can it be empty and flat? What could have happened?"

This so unsettles Eliza, she turns away and closes her eyes and only opens them again when she hears familiar sounds and sees her own Redcliff's Beach filled with hundreds of beach goers, cabins, homes, and three large resorts, all the things which makes this community so special to her.

The ponytailed woman pulling her wagon down an empty beach is nowhere to be seen. Scolding herself, Eliza growls, "Get a grip old girl, you're falling apart. Forget the Grand Jury, forget that whole week. Even the damn DA telling me murder cases never close. At least I had the sense to snap back, 'Good. Then maybe you'll catch the bastard who did it,' and looked at Mike. Damn it, I did what I had to do and I'm glad I did it. Good riddance to bad rubbish. From now on, I'm going to concentrate on meeting the women who share my place and let them prove I'm not crazy."

However, as Eliza walks through her slider door, Liz Day is slipping on a windbreaker and Eliza touches the woman's arm. "Hi Liz. I've decided you're right, we need to get to know each other. Would you to join me at the table?"

However, Liz does not react to her question and goes out the door and closes it. Irritated, Eliza mutters, "Well, hell, I finally want to talk to her and she ignores me. What went wrong? Damn, maybe I shouldn't have been such a shit to her before."

Around five that afternoon, the other woman, named Beth, walks through the front door and the room changes. This room looks washed down and Beth says something about workers who'd done the work. Puzzled by the look of the room, Eliza sits on one of her dining chairs and leans on the table to watch this Beth hurry back out the door. In a few minutes, Beth comes in carrying a large heavy looking piece of stone in her arms. Setting it on her dining table, she ignores Eliza's presence and pushes the stone to the center of the table. When she tips the stone, Eliza see it is a large translucent stone shaped into a bowl.

When the stone bowl is centered on the table, the large translucent stone in the floor begins to glow brightly as if greeting the stone centered on the table. Soon, both translucent agates are pulsing with a brilliant light and Eliza gasps as she sees the two agate shapes look as if made from the same stone.

As the lights become brilliant, Liz appears at the other end of the adjoined tables. However, the three women are so stunned by the pulsing lights, they don't react at the others seated near them. Suddenly, Beth speaks sharply and the lights dim. At that time, both Beth and Liz vanish from Eliza's home and she is seated at her table completely alone.

This time Eliza feels as if she is missing something wonderful. Shaking her head, she mutters, "I can't believe I'm missing people I don't even believe are real. If they are, we'd have to be clones and they don't allow human cloning. At least I don't think they do. Still, how else could the three of us be so alike? In this world? In this Universe?"

Slapping the table top, Eliza shouts, "Holy cow, I think I know what we women could be. I read about some sort of metaphysical paranormal phenomenon in that book Marie gave me last Christmas. What is the title of that book? Something about metaphysical events documented as being factual. There was a whole section on quantum leaps and string theory and dimensions of Universal Plains. It told about causes and effects of joined energy of such intensity that it causes life extensions from one being to reveal themselves to like-kinds.

"Maybe that's what we are, like-kind lives or whatever the name for that is. Hmmm... some sort of multiple dimensions? No.no... that Liz said her dead husband Peter told her, we were some kind of lives, but what? Split lives?

"Damn, I wish Marie were here. She loves this sort of stuff. Goes to hear others channel ancient entities who take over their bodies. Where did I put that book? I wouldn't have dumped it before my move up here, I'm sure of that."

As she talks to herself, Eliza runs up the stairs to her suite and goes to the bookshelves along the south wall. Running a finger along the spines of the books, she scans the titles as she mutters, "Marie tries to get me to go with her to have readings of my own. Now, I wish I'd gone last time, maybe someone would have told me something like this was going to happen. If so, I would have been more open to the women when they came to me that first time. In fact, Marie bought the book at one of those events as she knew my curiosity would get me to thumb through it. And I did... Ah, here it is." Eliza exclaims as she pulls a large tome off a high bookshelf.

Carrying the heavy book down the stairs, she takes it directly to her dining table and sets it down. Opening it to the table of contents, she scans down the list of chapters. Seeing the one she wants, she carefully opens the book to the page listed.

Parallel Lives (PL) page 351
Paranormal Metaphysical Mysteries

"Parallel Lives (PL) are entities which have split from the Original Life (OL). At that moment the PL becomes an entire new being within a new universal plain/dimension and each is unknown by either the Original Life (OL) or the Parallel Life (PL). These PLs split from the OLs during traumatic childhood events which the OL has no control of or is emotionally too young to handle. During these moments the child has no control over the separation which happens and is not aware of anything which happens. It is the traumatized child's essence which projects itself outward and away to escape from whatever event happens within the Original Life.

"These abrupt changes are not chosen by the OL but by the PL who projects itself away from the event to continue an existence it had been living or into another existence to avoid the trauma the OL experiences. The PL's split from the OL takes less than a nanosecond to form the chosen life path dimension. Both the OL and the PL continue living within their life path dimension unaware that any new life change was created.

"Within each life path dimension, created by a PL, the PL is as complete an entity as the OL within the original life dimension. Therefore, within their new life path dimension, PL's become an OL and PL's may split from it to create their own life path dimensions. This process happens whenever an OL experiences a traumatic event and the PL's wish to avoid the trauma. Thus, the PL's decision creates a life path dimension so instantaneously that neither the OL's nor the PL's are aware of the event happening. All Parallel Lives and Original Lives hold the exact same memories of the time they were one entity. It is only after the PL's life path split into its new dimensions when memories of the OL and PL become different as they are no longer joined within the same life. It must be remembered that the shared memories are the only holdovers when a new life path dimension is created by a PL. Afterwards, each life entity creates its own memories within its own dimension.

"However, each PL's new life path dimension retains, and carries forward, the essences of all loved ones, friendships and things which formed the world of the OL, especially the entities and things which are most prominent to make the PL's new life path dimension complete. This includes all things and people known by the OL. Each is brought forward within the PL's new life path dimension unaware of their original OL dimension as each continues within the live as they lived.

"As these dimensional life paths of OL's and PL's become separate dimensions, each continues to be tied by unseen energies connecting them to their like-kinds dimensions within the Universal Plain. These include all dimensions which have split from the Original Life born from the actual birth mother and those Parallel Lives which split from their OL/PL's. Only the OL and their PL's can become aware of or know the like-kind 'others'. This phenomenon happens only when there is a rupture within the Universal Plain (UL) which allows the like-kind dimensions to become connected through massive bursts of energies which cause a Quantum Leap through the Universal Plain to thrusts like-kind dimensions from their axis at the exact moment and to become tied at a focused axis point of which all OL's and PL's have a common knowledge.

"It must be emphasized that each PL is exactly the same, physically and mentally, as the OL at the time the new life path dimension is created. However, traumas and life style changes which occur through everyday conditions, such as illness or accidents or death, will cause change or damage to the entity who lives through those changes."

Pushing the large book away from her, Eliza feels confused by what she just read and she goes out the slider doors to the railing of her deck. Taking several deep breaths of fresh sea air, she rubs the goose bumps off her arms and stares north at the red cliffs, "Did I open the Pandora's box when I killed Jack? Is that why these women came to me? If not, why are they here at this time? Why now? Am I from one of those other women or are they from me? Who chose what and when? Was it when I shot that gun? Is that when they chose to leave my existence? No, that couldn't have happened then, their lives are too different from mine to have been created so recently. The book doesn't really say how or when new lives are created, only that childhood traumas create most Parallel Lives. Though it seems to say the cause could be anything, from life changes or illness, to family breakups or household moves. Most, I would suspect, would be due to the death of a parent or sibling or maybe even the Original Life."

Unsatisfied with what she read about Parallel Lives, Eliza returns to her table and carefully reads the chapter twice more. When she finishes this time, she wonders aloud, "Did Jack's life create a Parallel Life to continue to live in another dimension? Would it be a good and gentle life?" The thought brings a snort of laughter from her and she shakes her head. "Oh no, fat chance of that. The SOB would be the same in any life. Wonder where he finally ended up or, should I say, ended down? No, it would have been up, as God loves and forgives all his creatures, good and bad. Isn't that what we're taught?"

ELEVEN

June 15—Liz & Beth

LIZ and Beth have met at the adjoined tables every morning for the past week. Yesterday, after their morning run to the cliffs, they decided to try to meet at the cliffs and set their watches to make certain they left their homes at six AM and go directly to the cliffs. When Liz reaches the cliffs, she steps onto the granite slab and walks to the touchstone. Instantly, she is wrapped by a dense fog and she asks, "Beth? It's Liz. I'm at the touchstone." As she speaks, the fog turns deep gold and Beth steps forward. "Liz? It's me, Beth. I'm next to you at our touchstone. Do you see me? We're together, Liz. You are of me and I am of you."

As she speaks, the golden mist wraps both women in a blanket of energy that sends Beth's long pony tail straight up in the air and static electricity snaps wildly through it. With sparks shimmering glorious halos of light, Liz grabs Beth to her and yells, "Wahoo, you look amazing. Does my hair zap, too? And look, we didn't explode when I grabbed you. Isn't this great?"

Beth laughs, "Holy cow. Look at us, together at our touchstone, two Elizabeth Ann Andersons. You and me, side by side, at our touchstone in broad daylight. Who'd ever guess it could happen. Let's count to three and slap our touchstone together. Okay? One, two three..."

"I declare this run good and done!"

Both women shout as they hit the protruding translucent stone embedded in the face of the vertical cliff. Tears run down their cheeks and Beth's ponytail whips overhead as the static electricity encircles them with its streaks of lightning.

Seeing themselves in the other, the women whoop with laughter. Both for comfort and to hold onto their sense of reality they hold onto each other for a long time. As they release their other, the two step back yet hold onto the other's hand. For some while, they study the mirrored face before them and each sees the same arched brows, the same bright blue eyes, the same nose with the same number of freckles and the same full lips pulled into a smile so wide each shows the same looking teeth. Their grins look a bit clownish and causes both to giggle.

Finally, Beth exclaims. "Holy cow, Liz, we're too much. Could we be any more alike than we are right now? I could cut my hair, but then, we'd be so much the same that we wouldn't know which was which. Even the freckles on our arms are the same. Whew... I guess there's no way we can deny we're each of the other. This must be what identical twins feel."

"Oh, Beth, how right you are, we are too much. Do you have a birthmark on your knee? Yup, just like mine. Have you been seeing the one called Eliza Staples?"

"I've seen her a few times. The first was the day Maxine died. The woman ran into my house and out her entry door. Since then, we've bumped into each other, literally, a few times. However, she's so spooked by me that I got tired of trying to talk with her."

Liz agrees, "Yeah, that's what's happened to me, too. Maybe by the Solstice she'll be used to seeing us in her home and she'll come to the adjoined tables and sit with us. For now, let's concentrate on us. Weren't you amazed when we discovered we have the very same memories of being a child? We remember the same things up to the accident when we were fourteen? That must mean one of us split from the other, at the time of the car accident. What we need to share, now, are the years since."

"I'd like to start, Liz. It got so late, last night, I didn't get to tell you about our families' car accident and how it changed my sister, Dee. Though the accident killed your parents and your sister, Dana, our accident was only a fender bender. My sister, Dana Marie, was thrown over the front seat and slammed headfirst into the windshield all because, she didn't like to use a seatbelt. The concussion she got changed her into a horrible person.

"It's also when she demanded to be called Dee instead of Dana. If I forgot and didn't call her that, she'd throw a tantrum. The folks took her to different doctors and none could find anything wrong with her. However, less than a year later, my folks had to have her hospitalized as they discovered what terrible things she did to other children and animals. My folks couldn't deny she needed more help than they could give her when several people told them what Dee had done.

"That summer, during the neighborhood's annual picnic, in the middle of fifty people standing around with plates of food, Dee took hers over to sit on the grass beside Dad's dog. As she ate, she petted the dog and fed it bites of food. The dog looked up sweetly at Dee and I remember thinking how kind she was being to the animal. Then, Dee jammed her dinner knife into one of the dog's eyes. The dog made only one sharp yip and died.

"At first no one reacted. We were too stunned. Then Dad grabbed Dee, who was still jabbing into the wound, and yelled at Mom to get her purse and keys. Then, he hauled Dee into the house, wrapped a sheet around her and tied her up with clothesline. Another couple went with them to be witnesses of what had happened and to make certain Dee didn't hurt them or herself. They drove to a sanatorium near Salem and signed her in for an examination, evaluation, and for several month's observation.

"Dee stayed there five years and only came out after her Doctor pronounced her well. That was Dr. Ed McGowan the man Dee married.

Mom and Dad wouldn't have her in the house, so she married her Doctor and became Dee McGowan."

Liz is stunned by Beth's story about her sister. "Oh Beth, I'm so sorry. I had no idea our sisters would be so different. My Dana was a wonderful sister until she was killed that day. Maybe it would have been better for your family if Dee had been killed too."

"Yes, I've often wished she had been, I have to admit. My parents suffered terrible guilt though they tried to make a good home for me. They were wonderful when I told them I was a lesbian and they loved Maxine instantly when I brought her home."

They are halfway home before they notice the golden mist is gone and both see the other's Redcliff's Beach and the differences of the beaches in their dimensions. While Liz's beach is abuzz with beach goers, Beth's beach is empty of people and flat and they stand for many minutes comparing what they see in one to that in the other. At this time, each of the women accept their other as a member of her family in every sense of the word.

Unable to be seen by others, they hold the other's hand and stop often to pick a pretty shell or an unusual pebble or a piece of twisted driftwood from the beach. Whatever it is, each looks it over, then one or the other puts it into a pocket or tosses it onto the waves. Whatever they are doing or saying, the two never let go of the other's hand.

When they are at the steps to their decks, Beth tells Liz about the storm and the cleanup crew and how Tom Ames formed the newly dozed sand dunes around her cabin. Liz explains the flagpole they had passed and the path through the dunes. Giving each a hug, Liz and Beth let go of the other's hand and in that instant each is within her own dimension at her own beach and hurries into her home to sit at the adjoined tables.

Liz goes to the fridge to grab a cola and takes it to the table to wait for Beth. Her pop is nearly empty when Beth's table adjoins to hers. At that moment, Beth sits on the chair closest to Liz, and says, "Hey, Liz, sorry I'm late. I really had to use the bathroom."

Liz laughs. "Me, too. Wasn't it amazing how our hair zapped and flashed when we slapped our touchstone together? Then it disappeared when we were almost back home. I am so impressed at what you did to reclaim your beach. Did you see that my beach is the same as it was when we were kids? Even though you told me last night that your cabin was the only structure left on your beach, it shocked me to see for myself. It's so hard to understand how Dad's cabin could have not been swept away in those terrible years. Is there anything left south of your home?"

"No, not a thing. It does have some dunes that start south of my cabin. I never gave that area a second thought, until last week, when I had quite an experience. It happened when I on the beach searching for my things that storm had washed from the cabin. Let me tell about finding this wonderful stone bowl..."

Liz is pleased to hear how Beth found the agate bowl and when Beth finishes, she tells her, "I saw you bring it into the cabin and set it on the table. I watched you spread your sleeping bag on your sofa that night. I wondered why the cabin had such a scrubbed down look. However, when the agates got bright, you snapped at them and your home vanished. Did you have to carry this heavy bowl all the way home? It's so beautiful. Do you hide it when you leave the house?"

Beth shouts, "My God, Liz, you saw me carry the agate bowl inside. Why didn't you ask about it last night? You see it now, don't you? Good. Isn't it wonderful? I'm getting information from it while I sleep, I'm certain of it. Don't ask me how that's possible, I just take it as a given. Am I crazy? Do you feel anything special when you touch it? You do? Great. That proves we're the same person."

Running the fingers of both hands around the smooth thick rim of the glowing agate bowl, Beth tells Liz, "I wonder why it was given to me. At the cliffs, I was told I was the original Elizabeth Ann Anderson, but why not you? Why would that bowl be given to me, if we were the same person for fourteen years, why not to you?"

Suddenly Liz laughs and points at Beth, "Well, my dear friend, don't you understand what being 'the original Elizabeth Ann Anderson' means? You are that person, Beth. You weren't chosen to find this amazing agate bowl and place it on your table, there is no other Elizabeth Ann Anderson who could receive it, only you. Why? Easy answer, Beth. This bowl had to be given to the one person who could bring it to life. That stone came to you, Beth, because you are the original Elizabeth Ann Anderson. Simply as that, my dear. You are Elizabeth Ann Anderson and the rest of us, Elizabeth Ann Andersons came from you or one of your Parallel Lives. That's the deal, kiddo.

"That's why the storm trashed your home, to send you onto the beach to go to the south cliffs. That's why the cliff opened and you saw the touchstone waiting for you to come to it. When you placed your hands on it, the bowl was given to you to take home and place it over the stone Dad placed in the floor of our cabin years ago. Now you are receiving information held by the touchstones until you were able to retrieve it. I am sure that's why we came together.

"That's why your beach was emptied of others and became so useless and isolated. The touchstone made certain you'd have the beach to yourself. That fact alone makes it a perfect place for the stones to be brought together and release the information to you. What a treasure you've been given. How wonderful it must be to be on the beach with no other person around."

Beth laughs, "Oh thank you, Liz. I was so uneasy about telling you what the stones told me that first night. When I woke with knowing I was that original child, I wondered how you and Eliza would feel about my saying I am the original child. When I first said those words aloud, they had such a factitious ring to them. I was embarrassed to hear me say them aloud.

"As for being isolated, only when Dee shows up unexpectedly. Her hubby, Ed McGowan, called early this morning to tell me she's on another one of her rants about the cabin. He told me to watch out for her. Damn it, Liz, I'm tired of fighting off that crazy bitch."

TWELVE

June 15—Eliza

ELIZA returns from her run to the cliffs and turns up the path through the dunes to her home. Stopping at the entrance to the suites built under the extended front deck to the house, she tries each door and finds them securely locked. "I tend to forget we added these suites under the deck for Marie's daughters instead of changing the footprint of Dad's cabin. Julia and Janice didn't expect to be included in the rebuild, but they'll own this whole property someday and these suites can be rented out to friends or others if they need the income.

Going up the steps to the deck, Eliza hears a loud snorting sound and looks across the deck to where a heavy man is lying on one of her chaise lounges. His head is turned away to the south and he snores loudly. Frowning at the huge stomach rising and falling with each breath, Eliza recognizes Mike Hartman. Walking to the slider door, she opens it and turns to shout at him, "Hey you! What the hell are you doing on my chaise lounge? Who are you and what do you want?"

Startled, the large man struggles to get upright looking dazed and embarrassed, "Eliza? That you? It's Mike. Eliza? Mike Hartman. Sorry, if I scared you. I fell asleep after I sat down. I came out to see you but you weren't home when I got here. Look, I need answers to questions I have about Peg and Jack. Have you got time?"

"Sure, Mike. I have questions for you, too. Wait right there and I'll get us some iced tea and brownies. We'll sit out at the table. It's too nice to be inside." Eliza smiles, as she talks to him, then waves to her neighbors, Al and Penny, sitting on their deck two hundred feet to the south. When she'd shouted at Mike, they'd turned to watch the interaction between the two people. Eliza smiles, waves again, then gives silent thanks for nosey neighbors, like those two, who never miss a thing on 'their beach'. The couple waves again, then return to their reading.

In her kitchen, Eliza's smile fades as she reminds herself, *I know nothing, nothing. Not one thing. I know nothing. Not of Peg nor of Jack. I know nothing. I know nothing at all. Do you Mike? Do you? Did you do it? Did you do it, Mike?*

The last thought brings the smile back to Eliza's face as she carries the refreshments out to the table on the deck. "Over here, Mike. It'll be easier to talk, face to face, here at the table. Have some brownies. I never do breakfast before my run and I'm starved."

"Can I help?" Mike asks, as he lunges his heavy body off the chaise and thuds across the deck to the table.

Sitting in the shaded area under the deep eaves, Eliza stuffs a brownie into her mouth as she points at the plate and mumbles, "Have a brownie. Baked them fresh last night. Napkin?" For several minutes, neither speaks as they stuff the brownies into their mouths and drink the cold tea. Finally, the plate is empty and the two begin to speak at the same time.

"So, how did you…" "I want to know…" Then they stop and wait for an awkward moment to pass. Eliza flicks a hand toward Mike. "You first."

"Sorry to bother you way out here, but I need to know how long you knew about Jack and Peg's affair? That's why you left Hood River, right? It is, isn't it?"

"Good Lord, no. Never thought it and never imagined it. Not because of Jack, though, but because Peg professed to hate him so much. Said she hated how he treated me and was disgusted by all his affairs. I saw her last the day before I left. She came for lunch and planned to come over her this August for a couple weeks. When we said our goodbyes, she cried." Shaking her head, Eliza looks sad and bewildered. "No, never would I have thought those two would get together. Their deaths were a shock. Frank Gilbert came to tell me the day the housekeeper found them. When he told me what happened, I couldn't believe it. It's still very hard to think about. Neither one of them deserved to die that way. Even Jack, the poor asshole, didn't deserve to die that way. It's too terrible for words."

She saw the question in his eye and she laughs, "No, Mike I didn't shoot them. I was here, with witnesses all around me. People saw me on the deck and shopping in town. Everyone in Hood River may think I did, but it never happened. I hated what he did to our life. However, I was done with him years ago. I retired from Staples the first of June because I was tired of Hood River's gossips and I wanted to live at Redcliff's Beach. This is where I grew up. I came every summer, first with my parents and sister and then with Mina Staples. My life began and will end on Redcliff's Beach. No, Mike, I belong here at Redcliff's Beach and that's the reason I moved here. Staples Mansion holds nothing for me now that Mina is gone. After Jack's death was confirmed, I signed it over to the school district to be used for special events. I set up a trust in Mina's name for its upkeep."

As she speaks, Eliza watches Mike study her face. When she pauses, he touches the front of his shirt and taps his fingers on one of the buttons. Eliza laughs. "Why, Mike Hartman, I believe you actually want me to say I killed Jack and Peg. That's funny as I've been certain it was you who killed them. Peg was the only one in town who had the entry code to both the gate and the Mansion. She kept it in her address book right next to your kitchen phone. You knew it was there, though, didn't you, Mike?

"You ask why I didn't tell the grand jury or Frank Gilbert about that, I guess I figured since Frank was a friend of yours and Jack's, he would already know that fact and had decided to ignore it. I'm very aware of the good old boys' club that runs long and deep in Hood River. No, I didn't kill our spouses, Mike. It had to be you, I'm sure of it.

"You had to have known about Peg and Jack. Why else would you take up with that tart in New York City? Yup, Mike, you knew Peg and Jack were having an affair and didn't care. I can see it in your eyes, right now. Look at your face, you're turning beet red. Confess, Mike, you killed them, didn't you?"

Shaking his head frantically, Mike's eyes bulge from their sockets as veins pulse along his forehead, "No." he roars. "No, damn you. I was in Chili for two weeks before and in New York City on the day they were killed. Frank checked my alibi. I loved Peg. I loved Jack. He was my good friend."

"Yes, wasn't he? And Peg was your good wife. It must be a terrible thing to be cuckolded by your loving wife with your good friend. No sense crying about it now, Mike, it's out in the open and known by everyone. That must make it a thousand times worse. Yeah, you did it, Mike. You knew about them and you killed them. Come on, you can confess to me. Nobody will ever know. I'd certainly never tell. In fact, I say congratulations on doing the job so cleanly. I've spent many an hour trying to reconstruct how you did it. Where's the gun, Mike? Was it the one Peg found in a pawnshop on that trip to Denver, last year? Was it that antique pistol used by a real gunslinger? Yeah, that's the one. I can see it in your eyes. Quite a gun. A real six-shooter, as I remember. I'm right, aren't I? Mike?"

The big man stands so fast, he overturns the heavy bench where he'd been sitting and screams, "Damn you, damn you! I didn't have a thing to do with their deaths. You damn bitch. Why would you say those things? I loved Peg. Sure I had a fling with that woman, but I loved Peg. I never wanted a divorce. I would never hurt Peg for nothing. She was my darling, my friend. She was my soul mate."

As he shouts, Mike tugs his shirt front and three buttons pop off the front of it causing it to open. Instantly, Eliza sees wires and black chips stuck to a shaved patch of Mike's chest. When his fingers get caught in the wires, his gestures pull them out and he shakes them at Eliza, "Damn you! Now, they think I did it, you bitch! You confess or I'll kill you, too. Do you hear me? I'll kill you, too!"

At that time, Mike lunges across the table and Eliza throws herself onto the deck, screaming, "Help me! Help! Mike's trying to kill me! He's trying to kill me, too!"

In his fury, Mike pushes the heavy table over, grabs Eliza's arm and yanks her onto her feet. Pulling her towards him, she kicks at him, and manages to hit between the middle of his legs. When he grabs his groin and bends over, groaning from pain, Eliza twists to one side, kicks the back of Mike's knees until he trips and falls with a hard thud next to her. All the while, Eliza screams for help. After he falls, she crawls to the south railing, pulls herself up and frantically waves at the couple watching the action on her deck. "Help me, Penny... help me! Al! Penny! Help me! Call nine-one-one. Mike Hartman is attacking me! He killed Jack and now he's trying to kill me, too! Call nine-one-one."

Though the couple had been watching, they hadn't reacted until Eliza screams their names, then they each spring into action. Al races down their deck stairs onto a trail through the dunes while Penny dials her cellphone. Seeing their response, Eliza smiles and thinks, 'There's no better watchdog than a nosy neighbor. Thank you, Al and Penny.'

When Eliza turns towards Mike, she sees wires lying beside him on the deck. Scooping them up, she shouts at the black chips on the ends of the wires, "You can't hurt me, Mike! My neighbors are coming. They're calling nine-one-one. The police will catch you for killing Peg and Jack! Murderer! Give up murderer! Give up!"

Struggling to get his awkward body onto his feet, Mike staggers towards Eliza, swings his fists at her and shouts, "Damn you. Eliza, I'll be back and I'll kill you, too!" He swings at her again and, though he misses her, Eliza tumbles onto one of the chaise lounges and screams loudly for help. It's then that Mike sees her neighbor moving across the sand dunes and he races down the north side deck to the driveway to his car.

Bruised by her own efforts, Eliza hobbles after him. As she goes, she wraps the wires, from Mike's chest, around her neck and pulls on them twice to leave deep red marks that tell the story for her. As she does, she gags and coughs into them, "Mike tried to strangle me with these wires. My God, my throat hurts so much." She coughs as she talks to the wires, "That's why he hid them inside his shirt. Thank God, he's too fat and clumsy to move quickly or I'd be dead. I'll give these things to the Sheriff when he gets here."

Reaching the driveway, Eliza watches Mike's car spin its tires as it turns onto Shoreline Drive. Pointing in that direction, she yells, "Al, that's Mike Hartman. He's the one who killed Jack and his wife, Peg. He's the murderer!"

When Al reaches her, Eliza is sobbing loudly and he asks, "Who did you say that guy was?" he asks, panting to catch his breath. "Did you say that's who killed Jack?" Eliza coughs twice before whispering, "Yes. He killed them and said he'll be back to kill me." Holding her hand to her throat to indicate how badly it feels, she tugs at the wires twisting them even tighter. Taking her hands away, Al tells her, "Let me do that, Eliza, these wires are cutting into your neck. That stupid bastard. What a terrible thing to do to you. Don't try to talk. Hold still so I can unwind them and set you free. There you go, now breathe deeply. You're safe now. My God, he almost strangled you. You poor darling." As he takes the last of the wires off her, he puts a protective arm around her shoulders and Eliza leans against him for a few minutes, quietly crying into his shirt.

When Penny hollers from the top of the driveway, Eliza and Al step apart and watch her hurry down to where they wait. "I called the Sheriff. They'll get that guy. Shoreline Drives is the only road out from this beach. Did we hear you right? That's the man who killed Jack and that woman in your home in Hood River? Are you alright? I saw Al unwinding those wires from around your neck. Oh my, your poor neck is bleeding. We need to get those cuts cleaned off. Do you have anything in your house to use? Eliza? Are you going to be all right?"

Eliza whispers, "He wrapped the wires around my throat and pulled hard on them. I managed to kick him in the groin and he let go. Yes, it was him, Mike Hartman, who killed Jack and Peg. For some reason, he came here to kill me, too! At first, he said he only wanted to talk. I got us refreshments as I thought he was a friend. Then, he attacked me, for no reason. When he wrapped this bunch of wires around my neck, he was too huge to fight off. Then he knocked me down and I kicked his groin and his knees. All that time, he pulled on the wires around my neck and kept repeating, he'd kill me, too. When he said that, I knew he'd killed Jack and Peg. Al, Penny, thank you both so much. If you hadn't been here to help me. I don't think I would be alive right now. It's so wonderful to have neighbors like you both. Thank you, Penny and Al. Thank you both so very much."

Penny hugs Eliza and tells her, "You should know that he came here right after you left for your morning run. We saw him park in your driveway and we watched until he came back to the deck. Then he worked around the deck table and chairs as if checking them over. After a while he opened the slider door and disappeared inside your house. He was in there for over fifteen minutes. I timed him. Al had just stood to go check on him, when he came out to the deck, saw us watching him and waved with a big smile and shouted 'Hello'. We figured he was a friend of yours, so we waved and went back to our breakfast and newspapers. That was when he laid on the lounge and fell asleep until you came back from run. We could hear his snores clear over at our deck. As I said, he was inside your house for over fifteen minutes. Maybe you should check to see anything is missing."

"Thank you, Penny, thank you so much for telling me this. I'll go check things right now before our Sheriff gets here. That way I can report if there's anything's missing. Then, I'm going to lay down until the Sheriff gets here. I'm so shaky and my necks hurts terribly. Thank you both. I'm so very grateful you came to help me."

Then, Eliza walks directly to the north side deck and goes to the slider door. Under the overturned table, there are two more wires which she adds to the wad of wires in her hand. Carrying them into her home, she sets them on the table. Studying them closely, she smiles as she thinks to herself, *I was right, these are transmitters on the ends of the wires.*

Mike was bugged. Who would put him up to that? Gilbert? Could he be that stupid? What did he think I would say? I'm shocked that anyone would try such a thing. I'll give this mess to the local sheriff when he comes and let him handle Mike.

An hour later, the Sheriff has been to her house, interviewed her and took the wad of wires, studied them for some time, then put them into an evidence bag and left. Going up to the W's, Eliza watches the patrol car drive from her driveway to her neighbor's driveway. An hour later, Eliza goes onto the deck to sweep it off and sees the Sheriff sitting with Al and Penny on their beachside deck. The three are having a cold drink and talking animatedly. Seeing Eliza, Penny waves and shouts, "Come over for a cold one."

Waving back, Eliza shouts, "Not tonight. Thanks anyway." Then, she turns and finishes cleaning off the deck and turning the cushions on the chaise where Mike had slept. As she goes inside, Eliza remembers that Penny said Mike was inside her home for over fifteen minutes. That could only mean one thing, if he was bugged, he probably used those fifteen minutes to bug her home.

Going to the phone in the kitchen, she unscrews the mouthpiece and tips it over her palm. When a small black plastic chip falls out, Eliza is not at all surprised. Putting the chip in a pocket of her shorts, she feels along the kitchen counter and finds another black chip. Staring at the chip, Eliza frowns and begins a thorough search of her home, all the way up and through the W's and the lanai. When she is finished, she stands on the lanai and looks over the beach. In her left hand are ten small black chips exactly like the ones on the ends of those wires that Mike had tapped on his chest.

Eliza is uncertain that she's found them all. However, she knows what to do with these she's found. Taking a mug from the kitchen cabinet, she drops the chips into it and pours water over them. Staring at them, she is shaken by how easily her habit of talking aloud to herself could have nailed her for the two murders.

Shivering, she carries the mug with the chips up the stairs and into the powder room in the W's. Lifting the lid of the toilet, she dumps the mug's contents into the bowl and flushes. Watching the toilet bowl empty, she feels smugly satisfied. Then, Eliza takes her cellphone from her pocket and calls Frank Gilbert to tell him about Mike's visit. When the dispatcher tells her Gilbert is not in the office, Eliza tells her, "Have him call Eliza Staples. He has my number. Tell him, Mike Hartman came to my home and tried to kill me. The local Sheriff has taken my statement and the wires Mike tried to strangle me with. Two neighbors ran over her and saved me. Gilbert will know how to reach the Sheriff over here. Tell Frank to call me after he talks to him."

Less than fifteen minutes later, Frank Gilbert calls her and Eliza is surprised to hear his voice so soon. "Why Frank, your dispatch said you were out of the area. Thank you for calling back so soon. I wanted to let you know Mike Hartman came here this morning and attacked me. Yes, Frank, he tried to kill me! Yes, he did, damn it. He knocked me down and punched me, then he wrapped wires around my neck and pulled on them trying to strangle me. He'd hidden them under his shirt. The local Sheriff took them away in an evidence bag after he took my statement. If it weren't for my brave neighbors, Al and Penny, Mike would have killed me. He's your murderer, Frank. Said so himself. Yes, Frank, he did. Mike told me over and over that he would kill me, too. Too, Frank. Do you understand the word 'too' means 'also'? Also, Frank, also. Doesn't his yelling he'll kill me, too, over and over, tell you he was the one who killed Peg and Jack? As he ran away, he yelled he'd be back to kill me, too. That has to mean he's already killed and will kill me, too, if he gets a chance. I'm in my home with my doors and windows locked. My neighbors are watching my house from their home. Talk to the Sheriff, Frank, he'll tell you that they saw him attack me. It was terrifying! There's no telling what he'll do next or when he'll try to do it. I will. You take care, too, Frank."

As Eliza hangs up the phone, she smiles broadly, then says loudly, "Of course, it all makes sense. Mike killed Jack and Peg on the first of June. Who else could it be?"

By afternoon, Eliza realizes she won't relax or feel comfortable in her own home until she's sure every 'bug' is gone. Deciding there has to be some device to find them, she jumps into the Jeep and heads into Aberdeen to the electronics store. If there's anything that will find those devices, someone in that store will know what it is. *Doesn't every guy want to help a damsel in distress? I'll be that damsel distressed by a hateful ex-husband.*

After parking in front of the store, Eliza walks through the door to see there is only one person in the store with a clerk beside a cash register at the back counter. Though the man seems too young to know much of anything, Eliza looks him over as she moves across the room. *My God, he can't be more than twelve years old. What can he possibly know?*

With the thought still in her head, Eliza approaches the young man and clears her throat. When he looks at her, she smiles as she asks him, "May I interrupt you for a minute? I hope you can help me with a problem. You see, I need some advice, the thing is... well, I'm fairly certain that my house has been bugged by my ex-husband. Do you know what I mean? We're going through a rather messy divorce, right now, and he's determined to find something to use against me when we go to court. He won't admit that I'm the innocent one and he's the one who had a dozen affairs.

"The problem is, I keep finding small black plastic things around my house. One was on my phone and others were under counters. This morning I found one on the chair next to the table where I eat my meals. When I showed them to my sister, she told me she was sure they are 'bugs', those things private detectives use to listen to what is being said without anyone knowing they are being listened to. So far, I've found eight and, knowing his determination, I'm sure there must be many more of them. Is there anything I can buy from your store to find these things?"

The young man's gaze never falters as he listens to her tale and when she finishes her explanation, he nods and says, "Yeah, I know what you need. There's an easy fix for that sort of thing. Do you have one of those an old-style cellphones? The flip-up kind sold ten years ago?"

Without speaking, Eliza pulls out her smartphone and shows it to him.

"Nope. That's too new. Won't do the job. Those don't pick up static or interference from other things. Follow me." The young man walks to the other side of the store where there is a large phone display and Eliza follows him. When he goes behind a cluttered counter, he picks a box off the top shelf and tears it open. Then, he pulls an old style phone out, flips it open, and turns to Eliza. Handing her the phone, he says, "Here. This's the kind you need. Put the phone to your ear and walk around the store."

Eliza does what he says and hears a voice giving instructions along with several loud buzzes. "What am I hearing?"

"You heard that buzzing sound when you walked next to those radios? Do it again and hold it closer to them." Again, she does as instructed and hears the distinct buzz again. When he sees her surprised look, the young man tells her, "That's what you'll hear when you get close to one of those bugs. That buzz is electronic interference. You make calls to people then walk around your home holding that phone out to different surfaces. When you hear that buzz, you know you got a 'bug' nearby. Those 'bugs' are microchips that send messages. Don't get much call for this phone, anymore. Only sell it to old people. That's the last one and I won't order more. You can have it for ten bucks. I'll even set it up for you."

After the young man takes her money and hands her the prepared cellphone, Eliza pops it into her purse and says, "Thank you so much for your good assistance." Then, she leaves the store and heads Charlie back towards Shoreline Drive singing "I've got you now, you rascal you" as loud as she can.

As it's the middle of summer, the traffic is heavy and slow on the way back home. Patting the Jeep's steering wheel, Eliza says, "Hell, Charley, I could walk faster than this, but I don't blame you. Everyone wants to spend time at our wonderful beaches."

Several times, the traffic comes to a standstill and she takes the phone from her purse and calls Marie for a chat. As the phone starts to ring, a loud buzzing sound makes it impossible to hear her sister's voice and she tells her, "I'll have to call you when I get home. Some wires along the road seems to be interfering with my phone."

Then she tips down the visor and sees a black chip stuck to the back of it. Yanking the offending 'bug' off the surface, she flips it onto the road amongst the slow moving traffic. Dialing 'O' she runs the phone over the dashboard as the operator asks several times how she can help. Only hearing a loud buzzing, the operator cuts her off and Eliza pulls into a side road and finds two more 'bugs' in the Jeep, one behind the rearview mirror and the other on the underside of the steering wheel.

Moving back into traffic, Eliza calls Marie again and tells her what's she's doing. When Marie tells her she hears some static on her end, Eliza holds the phone down lower and finds a black chip stuck under the dashboard. When her sister hears another chip has been found, she shouts, "Who the hell does Mike think he is, Sam Spade? This is the damnedest thing I've ever heard. Be careful, Eliza, Mike sounds completely off balance. Be sure to tell the Sheriff about these chips as soon as you get home." Eliza reassures Marie she'll be careful and the sisters say their goodbyes.

At that time, the traffic picks up speed and Eliza holds the last chip up to her mouth and shouts into them, "What the hell? Here's another of those black chips like the ones I found after Mike Hartman was at my house. He must have stuck them all through my things. Who would ever have him do that? Don't they know it's against the law? Even I know that. I wonder if Frank Gilbert would be that stupid.

"I hope I hurt Mike when I kicked his balls. It got him to let go of me and that gave me time to roll away. That kick may have saved my life as he stopped pulling on the wires." After saying that, Eliza reaches her arm out the open window and drops the chip on Shoreline drive.

After she parks Charlie in the garage, Eliza dials Staples Fruit Packing Company and asks to speak to the new CEO of the company. Certain he'll give her a long-winded update on how things are going under his command. As the man talks, Eliza goes through both cars, the Jeep and the BMW and finds black chips under the dashes and visors. Going inside the house, she hurries up to the W's to do a thorough search and finds it clean.

For the next hour, Eliza listens to the CEO tell her about his plans for Staples Fruit Packing success. Responding to him when necessary, she moves through her home, room by room, stopping only to pick off a black chip when she hears the buzz. Finally, she goes onto the deck and finds two 'bugs' under the edge of a pot of sedums in the center of the table where she and Mike ate brownies and drank iced tea. Losing her patience, she simply tosses the 'bugs' into the sea grass of the sand dune far below her deck

At this time, she realizes the CEO on the phone has become repetitive, so she thanks him for the update and says goodbye. Then she drops the old style cellphone on the deck and stamps on it with the heel of her shoe. Picking up the parts, she takes them into the house and dumps them in the trash container under the sink. Taking a deep breath, she faces the north and whispers, "I declare this run good and done."

THIRTEEN

June 15—Liz

LIZ goes into Peter's office and takes the envelop Bob Drake left off the desk top and carries it out to the dining table. Opening its flap, she empties the photos and passports onto the table's surface. Alexandria Petrow is in all the photos, doing different things in different places. Each photo was taken from a great distance and most show her in focus. A few are blurred or of her back or side or she's straining over something to watch some activity. In most photos, people around her are of different nationalities and in different cities.

Liz counts over a hundred photos taken without Alexandria's knowledge. The woman never sees the camera nor looks surprised. Very few were taken at close range or blurred by motion of either Alex or the photographer.

Several passports lay amongst the photos and each is as Peter's were, showing Alex's face with different hairstyles, glasses or not, with different names and addresses on each. After studying these, Liz sets them on the table and begins to separate the photos into like-kind piles. Doing this takes Liz back to her discovery of what Peter had really done all their years together.

Tossing the last passport on the table, she is suddenly anxious about what might happen tonight. "Let's face it, kiddo, you're scared stiff of that woman. How could you have been so dumb for so many year? It seems as if I had to be sleep walking to not notice all I've discovered about my darling husband and my good friend and neighbor. I'd have been happier if I'd found out about their having an affair."

Laughing at the thought, Liz shouts at the ceiling, "Well, Peter, I'm glad you never did that with her. God only knows, though, how many women you've left hanging on around the world. All wondering why you haven't called for the past month. Poor things."

Going into the kitchen, she washes her hands under the tap for a full minute as if having handled something rotten. After drying them, she begins to mix up a double batch of brownies from the recipe she uses and turns on the oven to preheat. After buttering the baking dish, she scrapes the batter into it and spreads it evenly over the bottom. Setting the bowl into the sink, Liz adds soap and fills the dish to the rim trying not to think how things are planned to happen or what could go wrong.

When the oven dings, Liz places the baking dish on the middle rack and sets the timer. Then she fills a glass with iced tea and takes it out to the deck table to watch the setting sun spread brilliant color along the horizon. Splashes of gold, reds, and orange top incoming waves then turn the sand dunes pink with purple shadows.

The beauty of the moment is lost as Peter's lies fill Liz with anger. "Who was that man? What was I to him? Bob deceived me then. Maybe he plans to let Alex kill me tonight as I know so much about what they did and didn't do. Why am I helping him catch Alex? I should warn her. That's what a good friend would do. Why should I care if she was the one who shot Peter's plane? I never knew the man."

It is the oven timer that brings her back to the present and Liz hurries into the kitchen, opens the oven and slides the hot baking dish onto a cooling rack next to the sink. As she shuts off the oven, she sees by the stove's clock that it's time to make the first call to Alex. Again, Liz wonders why she is doing this for Bob's Company. Looking out the north window, Alex's house doesn't show any lights. In fact, it looks as if no one is there. "Is she even home?" Liz muses.

Poking at Alex's number in her cellphone, she walks over to the north window and watches the house. As the phone rings, Liz rethinks the words Bob gave her to say. When voicemail picks up, Liz says, "Hey Alex, I made a batch of brownies and know how much you love them. Come on over and let's have a real gal-pal talk. It's been too long."

Setting her phone on the counter, Liz wonders if Alex is still her friend or if she's now her enemy. "Maybe Alex fled Redcliff's Beach as Peter told her to do. Will she just come over to visit or just to kill me?" A chill crosses Liz's shoulders and she hugs herself, trying to hold off the thought.

An hour later, when the mantle clock chimes ten times, Liz redials Alex's number and again the voice mail picks up. Again, Liz repeats words Bob had given her to say. "Hey, Alex, come on over and let's talk. The brownies have cooled and the coffee is strong and hot. Come and let's talk. I need to know what you want me to do with an envelope I found in Peter's office today. It was tucked in the back of a drawer and is full of photos with you in them.

"I figured you might want to have them. If you don't call or come over tonight, I'll keep them until you let me know. I can dump them in the trash or burn them, whichever you'd like me to do. At the least, give me a call back and let me know one way or the other? I sure hope to see you tonight. I'm watching TV until eleven then I'm off to bed."

After she hangs up, she checks the slider door to make certain it's unlocked, then she goes into Peter's office and calls Bob Drake as he'd told her to do. When he answers, she tells him, "I left your messages. Alex's house is very dark. I think she may have left Redcliff's Beach for good."

"Alex is home and got your messages. Stay put. Don't call again. She'll be there soon enough. Don't leave the house and don't panic. We're close by. Do what I told you. Go behind your kitchen counter, cut brownies or whatever you can. Just look as if you're working at what you'd do anyway. Stay there, no matter what. When she comes, she'll have a gun. When she confronts you with it, drop to the floor behind the counter and roll to the far side. No ad-libbing, Liz. Say your lines and drop. You hear me?"

"Yes, Bob, I hear you. Be on time, that's all I ask." Not saying good-bye, Liz lays the phone on the desk top and hurries back to the kitchen. Touching the brownies, she feels they're cool enough to cut and lays each carefully on the large plate she set on the counter. Then she starts the coffee maker and sets two mugs next to it with the sugar and creamer nearby. Then, she washes the mixing bowl and baking dish in the sink and the warm water and doing something so ordinary, calms Liz.

Staring out the window over the sink, she hums an old tune and a rush of sadness sweeps over her. When tears fill her eyes and she blinks them away as she thinks, 'My life has changed too fast. Peter's death and finding I never knew him was horrible. As if those weren't enough to knock me off balance, two of my Parallel Lives have come to me and, now, I'm waiting for my friend to try to kill me. What the hell am I doing?'

Watching lights along the south beach, Liz whispers, "Please, let Beth and Eliza stay in my life forever. Next week is the Summer Solstice. Keep us tied to each other at the adjoined tables. I need both of these women in my life."

Wiping her hands on the dishtowel, Liz feels a breeze brush her cheek and she turns to see the slider door is wide open. A black shape is moving to the dining table and Liz recognizes the tall exotic looking woman dressed totally in black clothing: hooded sweatshirt, slacks, gloves and shoes. Alexander Petrow ignores Liz's presence until she pokes through the stacked photos and passports for several minutes. The woman studies each photo and passport carefully, then casually flips them to the other end of the table. When she is done with the last photo, she turns to face Liz.

The silence becomes surreal to Liz and she laughs loudly, "Good God, Alex, you look amazing, just like a character in that old Hitchcock movie. You know the one that Cary Grant romances Grace Kelly? Are you going to a costume party as the cat burglar/jewel robber? You're sure to win the prize if you are."

Without answering, Alex picks up two of the passports and opens them again. When done, she slaps them onto the table top and begins to talk to Liz without looking at her. "My, my, Liz Day, where did you ever get all these? Was this part of Peter's collection or did you get these yourself? Ah, no, I see, it had to be Peter's work."

Suddenly, Alex looks directly at Liz and sneers, "Elizabeth Ann Anderson, alias Liz Day, we've come to a sharp bend in the road of our long friendship, haven't we? No? Of course. You are so right, and I have to agree, this is no bend, this is the end of a great relationship. Right? Not a friendship? Well, what would you call it? More importantly, what are we going to do about it? Huh? Cat burglar got your tongue?"

Alex's laugh is ugly and loud as she pulls a long nosed pistol from under the hooded sweatshirt and Liz sees a long silencer attached to the end of the gun's barrel. Wide-eyed at the reality of the moment, Liz knows she should duck behind the counter, yet she can't seem to move and openly stares at the pistol as Alex waves it back and forth.

Watching the gun's effect on Liz, Alexandria laughs, "Tell me, my friend, are you prepared for my ending to our friendship? Or do you have plans to write your own ending?"

Liz answers with a sneer and repeats the words Bob Drake told her to say, "Why, Alex, Peter was right all along, wasn't he? He figured you were sent here with the Kremlin's blessings. How else could you live so openly, when hundreds of others had to hide in order to stay in the States? When the Soviet Union broke apart, you neither cheered nor shed a tear. Only a halfhearted vodka toast to the new Republic. Who pays for your fine lifestyle, Alex? Really? You certainly aren't that good of a clairvoyant." The last words are her own and when she sees the gun stops waving, she knows she has again said too much and starts to duck behind the counter.

Instead of shooting her, Alex sets the gun down on top of the photos and sits in a chair at the table. "Aw, Liz, that's your biggest problem, you're always too curious. You ask too many questions. Where'd I been, with whom, and why did I go? Oh my, you prattled on and on. Let me tell you, dear friend, I work for many and any. If the price is right, the deed is done. However, I digress, the immediate problem is what to do about you and these. I've delighted in our friendship over the years and it breaks my heart that it must end. You are the one person I allowed to come close to me and I was wrong to do so. My old Soviet friends are business partners and one should never get close to business partners. Don't you agree?

"However, I can't have you telling one and all what you've found out about me. Neither can I leave this evidence in your keeping. These passports I lost on some of my first trips after I moved here. At that time, Peter seemed to be wherever I went. It never dawned on me that he was more than a bean counter for his company. So, here we are, my friend, it's time to end this. Too bad for you and very bad for me. I've loved living at Redcliff's and knowing sweet gullible you. I thought you actually believed those tales I told about my clients. As for my being clairvoyant, I have many rich, famous clients who use my services to plan their future or the futures of others and there are several ways to do both."

In one swift movement, Alex grabs the pistol and aims. In that instant, Liz drops to the kitchen floor, a second before the first shot is fired, and shouts, "If you're so clairvoyant, Alex, why don't see the agents' guns pointed at you." When Liz flattens against the base of the cabinets, there are three rapid pops that send tiles flying off the backsplash behind the stove. Shaken, Liz knows, if she had not dropped so quickly, any one of those bullets would have killed her. Lying still as a stone, two loud shots ring out and, a second later, one pop from a gun with a silencer.

Then heavy footsteps shake the floor of the Liz's home. Squeezing her body closer to the baseboard, Liz does not move or breathe. Only when steps move into the kitchen and stop next to where she lays, does Liz hear Bob's voice. "Liz? You okay? Liz?"

"Yes, Bob. I'm fine. I'm too weak to stand and I peed my pants."

His chuckles cause her to blush as she lets him lift her to her feet. Looking up at him, Liz manages a weak smile, though, it vanishes when she sees three people working over something on the floor next to the dining table. Liz knows it is Alex and she looks the other way as Bob leads her to Peter's office.

"Did you kill her?"

"No, we shot her legs to get her down. She put the last bullet in her own head."

"She knew you were close, yet she came to kill me. Why?"

"You knew her too well, Liz. She let you get too close and then you betrayed her or so she thought. Her sort doesn't want anyone knowing too much about them. The man at her house was arrested as soon as she left to come over here. Border agents caught another of her cronies using a phony passport. We don't know how big Alex's gang was or even if it was. Stay here until I come back for you."

As he steps out the office door, Liz hears him tells the others. "File the evidence and finish the floor. I'll clean up the table and meet you in Seattle by twenty-four hundred. I'm out of here as soon as you're done."

Walking to the office door, Liz watches Drake stuff photos and passports into the manila envelope, seal it and turn to carry it back to where he left her. Seeing Liz watching him, he studies her face for several seconds. Then, without a word, he walks past her to Peter's desk and opens each desk drawer. Carefully feeling the inside of each and finds nothing more. Looking up at Liz, he studies her face. Frowning at him, she mentally denies having what they both know that she found.

Finally, he picks up the manila envelope and says, "You can dispose of anything in here you don't need or want. Peter had more passports with packets of money then he'd ever needed, both in the metal boxes and the manila envelopes. Several were for the same South American country. Each had a different name and disguised photos. He may have seen those as his only safe way out. I don't know why he'd think that, but he must have. We also found several bank books from closed accounts around the world. We're not certain if the money belonged to him or the Company. Do you know anything about a large amount of money?"

"No, Bob, I don't. I didn't open the envelopes only the two metal boxes. The only accounts we had together are with our financial advisor, who holds our investments, and our local bank which has our checking account and safe deposit box. I emptied the safe deposit box after Peter's death to get things for our tax accountant. I'm stunned to hear about the money and other accounts, but not surprised. At this point in time, there is nothing about Peter that would shock me more then I already have been."

When three people pass the office doorway carrying a black body bag, Liz watches them go out the front door and Bob follows them out the door. Stopping on the threshold, Liz watches the body bag vanish into the back of a black van. Shaking her head, Liz whispers, "Poor Alex, she must have been so lonely."

FOURTEEN

June 15—Beth

BETH hears the house phone ringing as she's opens the slider door but by the time she lifts the receiver the ringing has stopped. Hearing the beeps which indicate messages have been left, she dials the number to listen to them. There are three. The first is a reminder from Tom Ames that he'll be back in the morning to finish the dunes closest to the north cliffs. The second message is from Dee, who screams that Beth is to send her daughter, Nicole, back home as she is a very sick child. The third is from Nicole who says she's coming to the cabin to talk to Aunt Beth about some important things.

Hanging up the phone, Beth wonders about what she's heard, "Obviously Dee's having one of her manic rants. I wonder what she's did that would send Nicole way out here. What could that child have to talk to me about? I've had less than an hour alone with her since she was born. Dee made certain of that."

Opening the fridge, Beth pulls a bowl of tuna salad onto the counter and slaps a glob on a small plate, pours a glass of milk and takes both to her dining table. As she's finishing her food, she hears a soft tapping noise and stops chewing to listen. When she hears nothing, she takes her plate to the kitchen sink and rinses it. Then a knocking sounds on the front door and she goes to answer it. When there is nobody there, Beth goes back to the table. As she starts to sit, a loud rapping comes from the glass slider door. Turning to look out, Liz only sees a silhouette against the sunset. When the rapping starts again, Beth opens the door and sees it is her niece. Nicole. "Aunt Beth, it's me, Nicole, can I come inside?"

Opening the door wide, Beth exclaims, "Of course, it's you! I couldn't see against the sunset. However, I should have guessed it would be you. Welcome, darling girl. What are you doing way out here? I got your message right after your mom's. What's going on? Why come way out here to see me? Come, sit at the table. I just ate my dinner. Have you eaten? No? I have fresh bread and tuna salad. You can make a sandwich if you'd rather have it that way. What do you drink? Cola, milk, or water?"

"Yes, to the food and a cola, please. Thank you, Aunt Beth. I'm starved." Nicole answers as she sits at the table with straight-backed formality.

Beth gets two colas from the fridge, sets one in front of the young woman who pops the tab and takes a long drink. Seconds later, Beth returns with a plate of tuna salad with thick slices of bread on the side, "Eat up, kiddo. There're more if you want it."

Nicole opens her mouth to speak.

"No, eat first then we'll talk." Beth says as she pops the tab on her own can of cola and sips. When Nicole finishes the first sandwich, Beth is amazed when the girl makes a second sandwich and stuffs the food into her mouth.

Beth wonders, 'What do I know about this child? She's more a stranger than a relative, Dee made sure of that. What happened to bring her out to me? Why would she even think to come to me? Dee must have done something horrid.'

Finally, Nicole finishes her food, wipes her mouth on the napkin and takes her empty dish to the kitchen sink, rinses it and puts it into the drainer as Beth had done. The girl's actions surprise Beth as they are automatic with almost robotic reflexes. Still at the sink, Nicole fills a glass with water, drinks it down, then, refills it, sighs loudly and brings it back to the table. Looking at Beth, she says, "Thank you so much, Aunt Beth. It's been a while since I ate food that good. Would you have any sweets? I always finish my meals with a bite of something sweet." Catching the surprised look on Beth's face, Nicole has the grace to blush. "Oh gosh, I'm too presumptuous. I'm so sorry. I'm just like my mom, I drop in unannounced, then ask for more food. I apologize, Aunt Beth, really I do."

Though surprised, Beth is also pleased by the girl's request and tells her, "Trust me, Nicole, from the little I know of you, you're more like your father, not your mother. And, as it happens, I baked a batch of brownies yesterday to keep my chocolate fix happy. How about a couple? And a glass of milk? Would that do you?"

"Absolute!" Nicole exclaims and a smile spreads over her pretty face for the first time since she entered the cabin. When Beth sets the plate of sweets on the table, the girl stuffs one into her mouth, chews and swallows. The second brownie is eaten more lady-like between sips of her milk. Then, as if just seeing the agate bowl sitting in the middle of the table, Nicole asks, "Where did you find this beautiful bowl, Aunt Beth? It looks as if it fell off that stone you and mom used to run to slap when you were kids. See? It looks exactly like the stone Grandpa Jim put in the cabin floor, the one under your table."

"Yes, they do seem the same, don't they? However, they're not from the same stone. The agate bowl was given to me a week ago. It was the day after a terrible storm that trashed my cabin..." Beth watches Nicole's face as she relates the story of finding the beautiful stone in the south cliffs. The young woman's eyes widen as Beth finishes and says to the young woman, "Okay. That's enough about me and the stone. Now, it's your turn to tell me what happened between you and your mother."

When Nicole tucks her head, Beth adds, "I told you there was a message from Dee before yours. Neither told me anything, yet both said a whole lot. You two must have had quite a row."

Heaving a sigh, Nicole gives Beth a steady look. "Our argument was a real dilly, Aunt Beth. First off, Mom hates I'm going for a medical degree as it takes years of schooling and internships. That sets back any chance of me popping out grandchildren for years, if ever. Mom nags me to date guys. Nancy got knocked up by her history prof and they eloped in March. Their baby's due in July and Mom tells everyone they eloped last summer. Aunt Beth, they didn't even know each other then. Must admit, though, the guy's a hunk and seems to love Nancy, so things are cool that way. Mom's got another generation on the way and a professor son-in-law to brag on.

"Things changed rapidly for me last week. That's when Nancy told me, she and her husband are moving to New Hampshire after the baby gets here. Her hubby's accepted the position as Dean of Students for some preppy college back there. Nancy's thrilled as it's about as far away from Mom as she can get and still be in the States. I panicked, Aunt Beth, royally. After they go, I'll be the focus for Mom's rants. I decided to tell her my darkest deepest secret while Nancy is still here to stand with me. So I asked to talk to Mom and told her my secret. I knew it would shock her so I asked her to sit and listen to me. Then, like a dummy, I blurted it out, 'Mom I'm a lesbian.'"

Beth stares at her niece without saying a word, then she begins to chuckle, "Oh, dear God, no wonder I got the call of wrath from Dee. She knew you'd head this way. Is this true, Nicole? Be honest with me. Are you sure about being lesbian or are you just trying to hurt your mother? Don't play games with me, Nicole. One thing I will not tolerate is your using my lifestyle as a tool to hurt your mother. If you're just messing with her, stop it and go away. I will not tolerate it, either. However, if you are lesbian and have decided to come out to your parents and friends, I will stand with you. Know this, Nicole, if you are coming out of the closet, the next months, even years, are going to be a hard adjustment. It's not an easy road to take. Many gays never walk the walk and play the 'I'm straight' game for years, until the wall of self-contempt hits them. By then, many leave damaged wives or husbands dazed by their announcement. Others end their lives rather than make the choice you're making."

"Aunt Beth, even though Nancy and I are identical twins, I've known I was different from her all my life. When we were teens, we were both chased by boys, but she was the boy crazy one. I had lots of girlfriends with one boyfriend who later came out gay. When I was fourteen, it was Nancy who told me who I am. She's the best sister and friend anyone could ever have. I'll miss her terribly when she moves east. I told my Dad and friends years ago. To my surprise, they said they'd known it for years and had accepted the fact. It felt so great to finally tell Mom, but as soon as I told her, she totally rejected me.

"I left that house and moved to an apartment near UW where my internship is. It pays a bit of salary and Dad said he'd back me the rest of the way. He kept my secret for years as he knew how Mom would react." The young woman takes a deep breath and asks, "Could I stay here tonight, Aunt Beth? It's getting so late and I hate driving alone in the dark."

"Of course, Nicole. Stay as long as you like. However, you must let your parents know where you are. Do you have a cellphone? Good, call your father and tell him you're here and that I'll help you any way I can. My advice about Dee is to give her time. She's shocked and hurt. Most parents of gays decide their love for their child is stronger than any disappointment they may have. Your mom loves you. She'll come around, give her time. Tell me, how did you and your mom end things?"

"She shouted that I was no longer her child and stormed up the stairs to her room. I followed and tried to talk to her but she wouldn't let me into her bedroom. After an hour of pleading, I packed everything into my car, including my cat Dandy-lion. I couldn't leave my sweet kitty with that wicked witch, could I?" A crooked smile crosses Nicole's face and she begins to cry. "Aunt Beth, it was awful. I love Mom and she hates me and now I need a place to leave Dandy-lion. Could Dandy stay here with you, for a while? I can't have her at my apartment. She's a good kitty and I'll take her back as soon as I can. I don't want to lose her, too, Aunt Beth. Can she stay with you?"

Beth laughs, "You know what, Nicole? I was just telling a friend that I needed to get a pet. I'd love Dandy to stay with me and I'll keep her for as long as you like. I warn you though, she may want to stay forever once she sees what a lovely sandbox the beach is. Is she out in your car?"

Nicole nods.

"Go bring her inside."

"Thank you, Aunt Beth, thank you, so much! You don't know what it means to me to hear Dandy-lion has a home and you'll stand by me. I've felt so alone and scared since Mom turned on me. You'll love Dandy and I brought her bed and litter-box in the car."

"Nicole, darling girl, my parents were so opposite of the person Dee has become. They would love you no matter what you were, just as they loved me when I told them I was lesbian. Dad said to keep safe and stay proud. They never said a negative word. When I took my partner, Maxine, home to meet them, they loved her simply because she loved me. Let's give Dee some time. She could surprise us and turn out to be a good witch, after all.

"Now, go get Dandy. Then take a jacket off one of the hooks in the hall and go for a long walk on the beach. That always clears the cobwebs from my head. I'll call Dee while you're on the beach to let her know you're here. Unless you want to call her, yourself."

"Thank you, Aunt Beth. I'd like Mom to know I'm safe, but I'm not ready to hear any more negatives from her. Thanks for the loan of a jacket, all I wore is my sweater." Nicole grabs a windbreaker off a peg and runs out the door. Within minutes, the cat's litter box and cat-carrier are in the guest room. Putting the bag of cat food in the pantry, Nicole then places the cat's food and water dishes in a corner of the kitchen floor. Then she says, "Dandy will be out in a few minutes to see you. Sing or something. She loves music and company." Then the young woman goes out the slider and runs along the edge of the waves heading to the north red cliffs.

Watching her niece run up the beach, Beth picks up the phone and dials her sister's number. The voice that answers rasps with exhaustion. "Yes? Who is this?"

"Dee?"

"Oh... you."

"Yes, me. I got your message and want you to know Nicole came here a while ago and will stay the night. It seems she's moved to an apartment which doesn't allow cats and needed a place for Dandy to live. Why she thought of me, I don't know. When she gets back from her walk on the beach, I'll have her call you."

"No, Beth, I no longer have any children. My daughters are dead to me. Nicole declared herself to be the same deviant as you and Maxine. Nancy has announced that she is moving to the East, as far as she can go. I will never see either of them, again. No, I have no message for Nicole. You win, Beth. You win. You keep Nicole. I never want to see her again."

"Dee, stop talking nonsense. This isn't a competition. You're talking about your daughters. You can't mean what you're saying. Don't turn away from them. Nicole came out to ask me to care for her cat while she's in school and Nancy's husband has a wonderful new position at a school back East. She must move with him. You love them and they love you. Be kind to them, Dee, and they'll come home often. What does Ed say about how you're treating the girls?"

"I'm leaving that bastard. He screamed that I was wrong to turn away from Nicole and reject Nancy. He says they need my love more than ever. Hah, hah, hah, what a joke. He told me to let the girls live their lives as they want. Doesn't he realize what sacrifices I've made to get them the best of everything so they can have the best lives possible? Ed's wrong. You're wrong. When judgment day comes, you'll all burn in hell. You hear me Beth? You'll burn in hell."

Before Beth can respond, the phone line goes dead. Laying the receiver in its cradle, she walks to the open glass slider and stares out at the beach. Tears slip down her cheeks as the realization hits her that Dee needs professional help and hopes her husband, Dr. McGowan, will sign her into the sanitarium again. With that thought, Beth feels something tickle her legs and looks down to see the up-in-the-air-hello-tail of a large orange cat. Leaning over, she lets her fingers trail through its soft fur as it circles her legs. When the cat feels her touch, it looks up at Beth with gold eyes and mews softly. Picking up the animal, she nuzzles into its neck and whispers, "Dandy, did you hear, Dana's children have chosen their own lives. They've made their escape. Now they have a chance for normal lives. They have their Dad and Nicole has you and me, Dandy. This is your home and we'll be here whenever she visits."

Looking up, Beth whispers, "Maxine, now I understand what you meant by my saving two small lives. Please, help Dee to love her children while they can still forgive her. Before she breaks their hearts. Oh, Dandy-lion, it's such a sad, sad thing."

Taking the cat out to her chaise lounge, she sits to enjoy the afterglow of the sunset along the western horizon and strokes the soft fur until both fall asleep. The beat of running feet awakens both Beth and Dandy in time to see Nicole turn down the north side deck, running towards the front of the cabin. Carrying the cat in her arms, Beth goes through the cabin to open the front door. Stepping into the carport, she calls out, "Nicole? Do you need any help?"

"No thanks, Aunt Beth. I only brought a backpack with a few things as I knew I couldn't stay long." When Nicole comes past Beth, she kisses the cat's head. "Thanks for the beach time, Aunt Beth. You were right. A hike on the beach is great think time." Scratching behind her cat's ears, she sighs. "You're going to love living here, Dandy."

"Glad it worked for you, Nicole. I called your mother and, yes, she is the most stupid person I know. Seems your father has moved out over how she handled your announcement. From what I could tell over the phone, Dee's in one of her deeply depressed cycles. Does she take medications for her bi-polar?"

"Mother on meds? Mother needs nothing, Aunt Beth. Meds? Bite your tongue!" Nicole sneers with disgust. "It's the rest of us who are the sick ones. You can't imagine how Nancy and I've kowtowed to her every whim and listened to her every rant. Aunt Beth, you can't even begin to guess how wonderful it is to have survived twenty-one years and become old enough to move away from her. Dad left her? Good for him. I pray he has many good, happy years in his future. God bless him, Aunt Beth, Dad is the only reason Nancy and I are the least bit normal." Nicole shakes her head as she takes Dandy from Beth's arms and kisses the cat's brow.

Surprised by the strong emotions the girl shares with her, Beth erupts with a shout of laughter which sends the cat springing from Nicole's arms. At first it runs under the sofa, then it slinks past the two women to go under the dining table where it lays upon the glowing stone in the floor and purrs loudly. Both women stare at the cat's choice for a nap. Then Nicole hugs her aunt, saying "Thank you, Aunt Beth! Thank you! Thank you!"

"You're so welcome, dear girl, it's truly my pleasure." Beth answers. Then taking Nicole by the hand, she leads her to the guest room. "Now let's get you settled. There's a small closet and a dresser for anything you want to leave at the beach."

Suddenly shy, Nicole sets her backpack on the bed, then picks it up and sets it on the chair by the dresser. Then, for the third time, she picks it up and turns around as if searching for something. Seeing her niece's unease, Beth takes the pack from her and says, "Dear girl, relax. I'll set the pack on the bed and you put your things where you want them, anywhere, as you want them. If they can be left here, do so.

"Then go fill the tub and take a long hot bath. Towels and toiletries are on the shelves in the bathroom. Go. Take your time, then get into your cozies. There are more brownies and milk. This is your home for as long as you want it to be."

FIFTEEN

June 15—Eliza

ELIZA pours a glass of half iced tea and half lemonade from the fridge in the W's, then she adds two full shots of vodka and two of bourbon and two of gin. Stirring the strong drink with a long handled spoon, she takes a sip and yelps, "Wahoo. This should cure my blues." Taking the tall glass out to the lanai, she sits in the wicker chair and watches the sunset color the tips of the waves. During the time it takes the sun to slip below the horizon, Eliza gulps down the tea and thinks back over the last few weeks.

'Time will tell if I got away with killing Jack. So far I've been lucky. If Penny hadn't told me Mike was in my house while I was on my run, I would have hung myself that same day. I've got to stop talking aloud whenever I work out a problem as, right now, there seems to be many problems that need working out.

'The first is to connect with my Parallel Lives, Beth and Liz. They were both at their tables this morning. However, when I tried to get through to them, they disappeared. Nothing I have tried has worked. Could this be my punishment for killing Jack? Will I always see my Parallel Lives in my home, but never get to know them. If it is, I hate it'.

Eliza downs the last swallow of her drink and snarls, "What sort of pity party you throwing yourself, Eliza Staples? First a slam dunk iced tea and now whining about what you did and didn't do. Next week is the Summer Solstice. Be at the adjoined tables tonight. Sit till they see you. Even if it takes all night."

Pushing out of the wicker chair, Eliza weaves her way to the stairs. At the top step, she knows the drink has hit her full force and, as she sways forward, she grabs onto the banister, takes one tentative step at a time until she's at the bottom of the stairs. By this time, her head pounds and she has trouble focusing her eyes. When she squints, she sees there's no one at the adjoined tables. Disappointed, yet determined, she wobbles over and plops into one of the chairs. When neither of the other women come through to Eliza after an hour, she slurs loudly, "Damn-zit, youse two. Where're you? I'm at table. Where shoe?"

Turning, Eliza tries to see out the slider door. However, it's dark out and she sees only her own reflection due to a bright light in the room. Standing, she moves dangerously unstable towards the wall where the light switch is. Flipping it, the room blazes with light and she flips off. Looking around the room, she sees the bright glow comes from under the table. "What-shell's under there?" she mutters bending over to look.

For the first time in her life, Eliza sees the agate in the floor is pulsing with a bright light that comes from within the stone. Curious, Eliza kneels on the floor and crawls over to the stone. Staring into the pulsating light, she rubs the surface and the more she rubs, the brighter the stone becomes. Finally, her strong drink and the bright light overcome Eliza. Closing her eyes, she lays her head on the glowing stone as if it's a pillow and falls asleep with the pulsing rays shooting between the tresses of her hair.

As she sleeps, the drink she'd consumed brings pangs and pains and retches that seems about to spew her nausea outward. However, each time there is a moment of eminent gastronomical eruption at the surface, the pulsing light forms a vortex which carries any foulness, from either orifice, far out to sea. Thus, when Eliza finally stirs again, she awakens clean and clearheaded with not one ache or pain nor pang in her gut. In fact, she feels reborn and runs up the stairs to her bedroom.

Stripping off her clothes, she steps into the shower, turns all six of the spray jets and lets the pulsing hot water rinse her body. After she washes her hair and body with the rosemary/mint shampoo, she feels ready for the day. Turning to the golden stone in the teal tiled shower wall, she shouts, "I declare this run good and done."

Filling the glass next to the sink, Eliza drinks the water. As she does, she hears loud laughter coming from her downstairs. Walking into the bedroom, she sees she'd left both the bedroom and bathroom doors open. Dressing quickly, she creeps down the stairs to where she can see whoever is down there.

To her surprise, both Liz and Beth, are at the adjoined tables laughing and chatting loudly. Thrilled, Eliza goes directly to her own table and sits on the chair closest to the two women. However, neither women notice her and the two continue telling about their experiences on their morning run.

Not to be undone by this fact, Eliza decides to respond as if they do know she is there. Soon she's making the same animated gestures they are and it seems as if her others include her in their conversation. Soon, she is so involved with what Beth and Liz are saying, Eliza begins to respond even though the two women do not really see or hear her and, for the next hour, the odd threesome chat across the adjoined tables. Each responding to whatever is asked and with Eliza happily adding her thoughts on everything,

This odd three sided exchange ends when Beth stretches and yawns loudly as she points at the clock on her mantel. "Liz, we've got to get some sleep if we're going to our touchstone early. I'm going to say goodnight and get some sleep. Next week's the Solstice. Let's hope that Eliza will come through to us by then."

"I'm sure she will. It's too bad she didn't come to the tables tonight. It was a lot of fun. See you at six, kiddo. To bed, to bed, sleepyhead." Liz answers. At the moment the two Parallel Lives leave their tables, they vanish from Eliza's home. However, this time, Eliza knows the women haven't forgotten her. Hurrying up the stairs to her own bed, she sets her alarm as she's determined to be on that run the next the morning.

SIXTEEN

The Summer Solstice—Together

LIZ awakens to stars winking in the pre-dawn sky and sees it is nearly five. Swinging her legs off the side of her bed, she shouts, "It's the Summer Solstice." Stripping off her nighty, she takes a quick shower. In minutes, she's ready for her run to the north cliffs with Beth and finally meet Eliza. Turning the doorknob on her bedroom door, it seems to be stuck. Turning it again, she yanks the knob towards her and feels her dimensions shift as it adjusts within the Universal Plain to mesh fully with other like-kind dimension at the focused point. After spinning on their common orbit, one after the other settles at the focused point and the dimension matches the movement of their others until each spins to a stop. Then, all mesh together as if one many layered dimension.

After this happens, there is a loud Universal click and bright flash of light. At that moment, Liz's bedroom door flies open and she's propelled through the doorway to run straight into Beth Anderson. Both women are shocked by the abrupt meeting and stagger as they grab onto the other, trying to stay upright and not fall.

Each is stunned, amazed and, finally, delighted to see their other within the adjoined space of their homes. Speechless, they can only stare at their other for several minutes. Finally, Beth hugs Liz and exclaims, "It is you, Liz, it *is* you! Are you in my home or am I in yours? I never ever expected this to happen."

Laughing, Liz, holding on to Beth, stammers, "Me neither, Beth, me neither. Isn't this amazing?"

"Sure is." Beth answers as she stares at how her cabin fits the space of Liz's house. "Look, our cabins have settled right over each other and we don't have those sparks flashing around us when we're close together! This is wonderful!"

"Yes. Yes, it's wonderfully amazingly phenomenally stupendous and very surprising." Liz laughs as she looks around the room seeing what Beth sees. "What a day this Summer Solstice is going to be. Do you think Eliza Staples will be at the tables? I hope she'll be with us."

As Liz speaks, Beth points at the adjoined dining tables. "Liz, Eliza's dining table is adjoined with ours. I see how her cabin is more open than ours but still each of our homes meshes to the others. In fact, they're so close it's hard to see hard to see where one separates from the others."

Liz laughs. "Yes, they look as if a set of how to do the same home three different ways. Some of her details are the same. Look at the three fireplaces, they fit exactly. Each of the stones are exactly the same."

Beth walks to her kitchen sink and sees Liz's remodeled kitchen sets within hers though the appliances are newer. Staring around her, she says, "Look, Liz, I can see through your space as long as it's the same as mine. Your stairwell is where my bedroom is yet we ran smack into each other. I now see your floor has changes and is more like Eliza's home. The stairs of both your houses took over my bedroom space. Your second floor might even mesh with Eliza's. You'll have to tell me if it does, However, we'll have to have Eliza take photos of her third floor. Do you see what I mean?"

"Yes, I do," yelps Liz, excitedly moving through the meshed cabins. She walks through Beth's bedroom walls as there is none in her own home. "Look. I can go through your bedroom wall, but I'm stopped by from going up Eliza's stairs as they don't mesh with mine. Even though we've adjoined, we're each contained to the space of our own dimensions.

"Oh, Beth, it's so lovely to see your cabin. It's as if I'm back in my Dad's cabin again. I know you added on the uphill side, but this area is exactly as I remember it. I wish Eliza were with us. It would be wonderful to have her see this, too. Maybe she'll come later in the day."

"Look, Liz. Eliza's over there, at her table. Eliza, can you hear me?" Beth asks as she rushes to sit on the chair closest to Eliza and touches the woman's hand. "You are Eliza Staples, aren't you? I'm Beth Anderson. The woman on your other side is Liz Day. Will you stay with us this time? Will you talk to us, Eliza? We're each from one child named Elizabeth Ann Anderson. At least, that's what Liz and I've come to believe. We want to know you, too, Eliza. Please, stay and talk with us."

Eliza stares at their faces, then without a word, she wraps her arms around the two women and pulls them into a hug. Surprised and pleased by her actions, the three Parallel Lives hold onto each other. While they cling together, there is a final adjustment made within the Universal Plain, which shakes the chairs they sit on so hard that the women have to grab hold of the adjoined tables to keep from falling onto the floor. When the shaking stops, the three are dazed and hold onto each other until there are no further movements. Then, the three women look at each other and burst into laughter.

Clapping her hands, Eliza yells, "What a trip that was. I'm so glad we were together when that happened, I don't think I'd have lived, if I'd been alone. Do you see how perfectly our dimensions are meshed together now? Much more than just a few minutes ago? Please, can I hold your hands? I need to feel you both are here and know I'm not hallucinating. For the past weeks, I've been so afraid I'd never get to be with you."

Liz nods, "We all need to hold onto each other and know we're real. Eliza, we're each a Parallel Life from one child named Elizabeth Ann Anderson. You should know something right now what we've discovered about Beth. Do you want me to tell her, Beth?"

Choked with emotion, Beth nods, "To put it briefly, Eliza, Liz and I believe that I am the original child and I'll tell you later why that is. However, we three are finally together and I want to know about you. Liz knows she split off me when we were fourteen and we both know why it happened. We also know that we lost our loved ones on the first of June. Because of these facts, we think it was those traumas which opened our dimensions to the other. We don't really care how or why it happened. Not anymore. We're just glad we're together. Will you tell us your story, Eliza? We'd like you to be in our lives. Will you, Eliza?"

When Eliza smiles at the women, her face is filled with joy. "Of course, my dear Elizabeth Ann Andersons. Yes. Yes, I'll stay and tell you all about me. Then I want to hear everything about each of you. I believe I have answers to what and why this phenomenon happened. My sister, Marie gave me a book on metaphysical phenomenon which talks about Parallel Lives. For days and days, I've sat here at the tables and watched you both. I tried everything to get your attention. After rejecting you those first days, I thought I'd never get another chance to know you. So I've sat beside you, here at the adjoined tables, many times talking with you both. This being the Summer Solstice, I came down to the table early. When you weren't here. I thought you were lost to me. Then our homes meshed and, poof, out of nowhere, you walk right up to me. How did you do that?"

Shaking her head, Liz laughs, "We don't know, Eliza. It just happens. A few minutes ago, Beth and I ran smack into each other outside our bedroom doors and mine is on the floor above hers."

Nodding, Beth adds, "Eliza, this Summer Solstice is one of the four days each year when the planets, stars and moons align within the Universe. We believe it is those times when like-kind dimensions such as ours are pulled apart to open to other like-kind dimensions. We tried everything to bring you through to us today and here you are."

Liz smiles at Eliza, "Please, tell us your story. Then we'll each tell you ours. Maybe then we'll understand why it took us so long to meet you. As Beth said, we discovered talking about our lives that we were the same child until we were in an accident when we were fourteen.

That accident killed both my parents and my sister, Dana. However, Beth's family's accident was a fender bender that shouldn't have hurt anyone. Except her sister, Dee, refused to wear a seatbelt as it wrinkled her blouse. She was thrown into the windshield and received terrible brain damage which changed her forever. She suffers as a bi-polar manic-depressive to this day."

Beth says, "That's right, Eliza, and I'll tell you about it. Right now, we want to hear about you, Eliza. Will you share your life with us?"

Eliza begins by telling about her childhood and how it differed from what she'd heard the others had experienced. As she comes to the time to tell about killing Jack and Pet, she pauses and takes a deep breath. Looking at the other women, she says, "Now, I'm going to tell you something which will shock you. Try to understand I did what I did as I was off my meds, I'm suffer as a bi-polar manic-depressive and was off my meds two days, too long. When you hear what I did, please, don't turn away from me."

Both Liz and Beth solemnly promise Eliza they would not judge her. At that time, Eliza quietly tells about the worst days of her life. When she finishes, Liz simply clears her throat and begins to tell about her life. When she finishes, Beth's tells about hers. When all the questions have been asked and all the answers are given, the three woman become silent. Finally, without a word, each smiles and stretches and yawns. Standing, they face each other and take the hands of the one beside them forming a tight circle.

Liz asks, "Do you understand why we feel Beth is the original child, Eliza? Her beach was emptied of everything except Dad's cabin and she was given the translucent bowl from the south cliffs. She is, so far, the only one to see the touchstones in both the north and south cliffs. Until that happened, both of us had thought it might have been you, as you stayed away so long. However, Beth's Dad took her away when your Dad was killed at work. When our accident happened, I went into a new dimension."

"Yes, yes. I can see what you mean." Eliza nods. "But could we stop talking about it? My head aches from trying to get ahold of all the information. I need beach time. Let's go slap our touchstone. After all, this is our first Summer Solstice and we should do it together."

"Great idea, Eliza. Let's do it." Liz exclaims as she heads for her slider door.

"Meet you there." Beth shouts as each opens the door out to their decks.

However, at that instant, three things happen.

One to each woman:

To Liz, the kitchen phone rings.

To Beth, someone pounds on her front door.

To Eliza, the front doorbell chimes.

SEVENTEEN

The Happening—Liz

LIZ has opened her slider door when her phone rings. Answering it, Bob Drake barks orders at her, "Don't talk. Go to Peter's office. Lock and bolt the door. Hit the red button on right corner of desk. Alex's people are on your drive. Don't hang-up, just go!"

On pure instinct to survive, Liz drops the phone, runs into the office, slams the door, locks and bolts the door. Taking the distance to the large desk in one leap, she hits the red button on the desk. Her actions take seconds, yet it seems longer and she throws herself into the far corner of the room. From there the desk shields her from whoever might come through the door. Her heart pounds loudly in her ears and she tries to calm herself as she scans the room for alternate exits. Seeing the door to Peter's bathroom, Liz feels the need to use it and creeps to the door and turns the knob. It's locked. Instantly, Liz realizes the office offers no other escape routes and fear overwhelms her as she rushes back to the corner of the room.

This is why Bob said the office was secured from outside entry if I needed a safe room. I didn't understand then, now I do. Peter was doing something that needed a room to protect him from intruders. Why didn't he tell me about it? Was he caught in something he couldn't change? Was that what the million was for? Would he have taken me with him? Now I'm hiding and I don't even know what I'm hiding from. Maybe it's the money I hid. Maybe it wasn't Peter's. Maybe it belonged to others who now want it back. Maybe Alex knew about it and that's why she wanted to help clear out his office. Maybe that's why she got mad when I turned her away after his death. Maybe that's why she tried to kill me. If so, why didn't Bob ask me for it? Or did he? Maybe he thinks I'm too stupid to have found it. Maybe it was both of their money and he wants his share. Maybe these people are really Bob's team. Maybe I know too much. Of what??

Fury rushes through Liz and she hisses, "Damn you, Peter Day, damn you. Why weren't you honest with me? Why didn't you trust me? Did your life have anything to do with me? Where the hell was my brain? Why didn't I question the locks on the door and your isolation in this room? How could I believe it was for protection against industrial espionage? That's the biggest joke ever as you never owned a company. Did you ever think I might need this safe room because of your business?"

Spitting the last words, Liz snarls, "Damn you, Peter Day. If I don't live through this, I'm going to wring your neck when I see you. It's the Summer Solstice. Eliza and Beth are at the rock wondering where I am. You bastard, Peter, you damn bastard. I'd better live through this so I can be with my others, or I'm going to haunt you forever, you damn bastard."

As if an answer, a loud pounding hits the office door and Liz opens her mouth to shout, then snaps it shut knowing Bob would use certain code words and rapping if it were him. From the other side of the door, a woman's voice calls out, "Hello in there, Hello? All is well out here. You may come out now, Mrs. Day. Everything is fine. Unlock the door, please, and come out. We need you to identify a body we have found."

Liz pushes herself into the corner and hugs her knees up to her chin. For several minutes, the silence hangs in the room as if a dead weight. Then something hard pounds on the door startling Liz and causes tears to slip down her cheeks. When the pounding stops, a deep voice demands, "Open this door, right now, you damn bitch. Come out of there. You can't escape from us. There is no way out. You must do as I say. Open this door." Hugging her knees tighter, Liz feels lightheaded and gasps with fright.

When she doesn't respond to the man's demands, there is another long silence. Several minutes go by, then a light tapping starts on the door. It stops and another knocking starts using a different patterns of knocking. Then a soft voice calls out, "Darling? Could you please open the door? Everything is clear now and you can come outside," The woman's voice calls sweetly to her. "Darling, please, open the door. Can't you hear me? Pretty please? For me? I know you hear me. Please open the door, Mrs. Day. We have Peter out here and if you don't unlock this door and come outside tight now, we will have to shoot him. Only you can save his life by opening this door. If you do, he will live, if you don't, he will die."

When Peter's name is used, Liz realizes these people don't know her husband is dead. Now, she wonders who is at her door and why. If they were part of Alex's gang, they would know he'd died in the plane crash. Clenching her teeth, Liz's fear turns to anger and she wants to shout at the stupidity of the intruders. Instead, she crawls under the large desk and huddles in the darkness. Settling into the space, Liz stretches out her legs and feels a bit safer.

When the hard pounding begins, again, she no longer fears the gruff voice which makes its demand. When the voice stops in mid-sentence, Liz becomes aware of some sort of rough activity on the other side of the door. Then there are shouted commands and gunfire. Then it is silent again. Then there are more shouts and more gunfire. Then there is the same eerie silence that happened after the shooting of Alexandria Petrow. At that time, Liz is certain that things have changed for the good and she slowly crawls out from under the desk.

Standing upright, she stretches each arm and leg and feels the relief of fresh blood reaching cramped joints. Sinking into the large black leather desk chair, she rocks and swivels gently as she waits for Drake's coded raps to tell her he's outside the door. Sighing with relief, she's certain Bob will come for her soon, if he lives.

For nearly an hour, Liz ponders all the possibilities which may have happened and, when Bob's rapped code sounds on the door, it has to be repeated five times before Liz believes what she hears. Then, it's when she hears his voice say, "Dakota Debbie Don. Is Elizabeth Ann Anderson in there? Is Liz Day? Liz? Bob Drake, here. Don't open the door, the cleanup is still going on. I'll get you when it's done. Liz? You hear me?"

"Yes, Bob, I hear you," she calls out, frowning at the word 'cleanup'.

It is another hour before, Liz hears Bob's coded rapping and his voice telling her to open the office door. Still, she waits several more seconds before she leaves the comfort of the chair and goes to the door. When she opens the door, Bob is standing directly in front of her. Without a word, she takes the one step up to him and he holds her for several seconds. Over his right shoulder, Liz sees the cleanup has been done and the sign of the struggle she'd heard through the thick door has been wiped clean. Pushing away, she gestures at the wet floor next to the table. "No tell-tale signs left behind?"

Bob nods, with a brief frown, "Told you before, not if we can help it."

Turning from him, she walks to the open entry door and watches his team load three people in black into the back of a black van. The back doors of another van are open wide and one body-bag lies on the rack inside. Then the doors on both vans are slammed shut and the vans drive away.

Bob waits until the vehicles have disappeared before he says, "This is need to know, Liz. Understand?"

"Goes without saying, Bob, I don't need to be told. The truth is, if you and Peter had trusted me, he'd still be alive as Alex would never have become my friend nor would she have stayed at Redcliff's Beach. So no more talk. Just go. I've a lot of thinking to do about who to let into my life. My mind spins with unanswered questions." Seeing a look in his eyes, she shakes her head, "Not now, Bob, maybe never. I need friends, not lovers. I need a big dose of truth with no lies or innuendoes."

EIGHTEEN

The Happening—Beth

BETH'S response to the knocking at her door is immediate as she assumes it is Nicole returning for another weekend. Pulling the door open, she shouts, "Hello darling girl, goo..."

However, it is not Nicole standing on the front steps inside the carport. It's Nicole's mother, Beth's sister, Dee McGowan.

Shocked, Beth shouts, "What the hell do think you're doing here? Get out of my carport and get off my property. The injunction against you says you're not to be this close to me and never ever on this place. You're trespassing. The Judge will send you to jail when you get arrested this time. You have a minute to get out of here or I call and get a warrant for your arrest."

A look of rage twists Dee's face as she rushes up the steps and grabs Beth by the throat, screaming, "You stupid dumb bitch, I'm here to kill you. Don't you understand? I'm going to kill you right now. You are dead meat."

Gagging from the fingers digging into her throat, Beth smashes Dee in the face with both her fists. Instantly, blood gushes from the woman's nose and she lets go of Beth. As Beth turns to run to the phone on the kitchen counter, Dee runs after her and Beth swings and hits Dee hard causing the woman to stagger backwards. Hitting her again and again, Beth punches at her sister until they are back at the front door.

Pushing Dee down the steps, Beth slams the door, locks it and yells to her sister. "Now get into your car and get the hell off my property. Don't ever come back here. Run like hell, Dee, I'm unleashing the dogs of war on you."

Having said that, Beth turns and rushes to the counter and grabs her phone and tries to dial nine-one-one. Suddenly, Dee rushes in through the open slider door from the deck and shouts at Beth, "Drop that phone, you bitch, you're about to die."

Running at her sister, Beth shouts, "Get out of my house, Dee. Get off my property." As the words leave her mouth, she sees Dee raise her right hand and point something directly at her. In the next instant, Beth feels three piercing hits across her body and she turns to run.

As Dee pulls the trigger, she screams, "Die, you bitching queer. Die."

The first shot hits Beth's right shoulder, spins her to face the dining table. The second shot tears into her left arm and its force knocks her face down onto the concrete floor knocking her out. She doesn't hear or feel the next shots. The third imbeds into the kitchen cabinetry. The fourth hits the arm of the sofa in front of the fireplace. However, the fifth bullet does the damage Dee had tried to do with the first five bullets. It hits the middle of her back, barely missing her spine.

As Beth begins to drift from her body, Maxine stands in front of her and stops her from leaving. *'Go back, Beth. This is not your time. Go back, my darling. You've a life to live. Others need you, more than I. Lay over the golden stone. Lay on it. The stones will heal you. Go lay to the stones.*

As Beth crawls to the stone under her table, her mind screams to her others, *Help me, Liz. Help me, Eliza. Come to me, I'm bleeding. I need help. I must live. I want to live. Dee shot me. The damned bitch, the damned bitch...'*

At that moment, Liz is walking to her dining table. When she is about to sit down, the light changes and she finds herself inside Beth's cabin. Calling out, she asks, "Beth? Are you here?"

As she turns to look around, her foot kicks something on the floor.

Looking down. Liz see Beth sprawled across on the floor with her head on the pulsing stone in the floor. The agate bowl on the table pulses bright light up across the ceiling. Beth groans as Liz kneels beside her and sees the massive wound in Beth's back. "Stone, need on stone. Help me." Beth whispers to Liz.

In one grand effort, Liz grabs Beth from above, then pulls the limp form onto the pulsing translucent stone. When the light shoots through the open wound the flow of blood stops. Almost instantly, the wound begins to come alive pulsing with the light rays coming through the hole in the middle of Beth's stomach. Then the wound visibly shrinks with each pulse of the light. Liz rips the T-shirt material away from the wound and lets the wound shimmer with the light. Then, as Liz watches, the horrific damages begins to close, from the inside out, until the ripped flesh has totally repaired itself and there is no evidence of the damage done by the bullet.

When Beth rolls onto her right side, Liz sees there are two healing wounds in Beth's left arm. Again, as she watches, these wounds close from the inside to the outside leaving Beth's flesh void of any damage from the bullets. As soon as the skin is clean of any wound damage, Liz sees, as if by unseen hands, the cotton material of the T-shirt becomes re-woven until the shirt is clean as if new. There are no stains or tears on the shirt.

After these miracles complete themselves, Beth wakens with a puzzled expression and she stares at Liz sitting next to her. "Liz? Why are we under the tables? What happened? Why am I lying here on the agate in the floor? I heard a knock at the front door and went to open it. I thought it was Nicole. Oh my God, I remember I opened the door and Dee was there. I fought with her and pushed her back out the door. Then she ran in through the slider door and pointed something at me. Was it a gun? Did she shoot me? I remember turning from her then nothing. I didn't see a gun."

Liz says, "Yes, you were shot. Three times. Twice in your left arm and once through your back and stomach. I don't know who shot you, but your wounds were deadly. When I found you here under the table there was blood all over. You evidently pulled yourself over the stone here under the table. There was a lot of blood and all your wounds were horrible. Blood was all over you.

"When I knelt beside you, Beth, You asked for me to pull you over the stone. When I did, light shone through your wounds and you began to heal from the inside out. You did, Beth. The light from your stones shimmered all through you and healed you. Their glow came in and out through your wounds and healed you. I know that sounds crazy but it's a fact. The pulsing light of the stone healed you within minutes. There is no other way those wounds would have been healed. You should have died. They were horrible. The hole in your back was the size of my fist and blood gushed from it. When the light hit it, the bleeding stopped and your wounds began to heal. All I could do was watch as the wounds healed from the inside out and close themselves. It was amazing. It was a miracle. What else could it have been?

"Look at your shirt. It's completely whole and totally clean. Nothing shows on it or your skin that there were any damages. I'm telling you the truth, Beth. I saw your wounds heal from the inside out. I saw your shirt reweave itself in the places where the bullets had shredded it. Now, it's as if you just put on a fresh shirt. That's what I saw, Beth, that's what happened. I saw everything as I said it happened. I can't believe your sister hates you so much that she would hurt you so badly."

Beth frowns and says. "Dee? Dee is not a loving sister, Liz. I told you how she hated Maxine and me and what we did with our lives. Of course. Dee, my loving sister, hated me enough to shoot to kill me. Where's my phone? I've got to call the Sheriff and tell him to bring her in. This time I will charge her. Liz, is my phone on the kitchen counter?"

Standing, Liz quickly gets the phone and brings it to Beth. As her other sits on the floor beside the table leg, she shows no signs of being shot or nearly dying. There is nothing left that shows what she'd been through the past hour. There is not a stain on her shirt nor a drop of blood on the floor. "Beth, how are you going to charge Dee with shooting you when you are healed? There's nothing to show you were shot or even wounded. Nothing. Your shirt is fresh and clean. There are no holes where the bullets went through it. There's nothing to show you'd been hurt. Nothing."

Without comment, Beth walks to her counter and lays the phone down and looks at Liz who followed her to make certain she is steady on her feet. Smiling at her, Beth says, "You're right, Liz. If there's no evidence I can't charge Dee with shooting me. However, I can sure charge her for violating the injunction." Having said that, Beth dials nine-one-one and asks the dispatcher to alert the Sheriff about Dee's visit. This time she asks for her sister to be picked up and held. "I'll be in to sign papers this time as I want to press charges against her. Please give the Sheriff my message. He knows Dee's history and will take the action needed."

NINETEEN

The Happening—Eliza

E L I Z A ignores the doorbell as she doesn't want to lose contact with her others and, after closing the slider, races down the steps to the beach path. At that moment, she hears her name shouted as footsteps pound along the north side deck of her house. Glancing over her shoulder, Eliza sees a man running at her with a gun pointed at her. Mike Hartman, his face twisted with rage, volts over the deck railing onto the path shooting in her direction.

Eliza throws herself off the path, dodges between the high grass-topped dunes, through the crowds on the beach and doesn't stop until she reaches the edge of the low tide. Focusing on the red cliffs to the north, she doesn't notice the people she runs past, nor does she see these people do not watch her run past them. The crowded beach has turned in mass to face the house where several shots can still be heard. The only thing Eliza knows is that if she stops she will die. So she runs north with one thought, *'If this the last day of my life, I will end it at my touchstone with my others.'*

Repeating these words, she reaches the base of the cliffs and staggers onto the granite slab and slaps at the translucent stone in the vertical cliff face and cries, "I declare this run is good and done." Looking around the area, she sees that most of the beachgoers around the cliffs are running towards shore yet some are running towards the south.

"Beth? Liz? Are you here? It's Eliza. I'm here. Mike Hartman shot at me and I ran here to be with you. Where are you?" When her others do not appear to her, Eliza slaps the protruding stone and shouts again, "I declare this run is good and done."

Turning to the beach, she sees there is now no one near her at the red cliffs. In fact, the few people left are either moving off the beach or towards a large crowd gathering where flashing lights can be seen along Shoreline Drive. "My God, those lights are at my house. If the cops are there, Mike is either still shooting or dead. Damn, I hope it's the last as I don't want to go to court and testify against him. Damn Gilbert for not believing me about his saying he planned to kill me. His death sure would make things easier for me."

Sitting on the edge of the granite slab, Eliza feels lightheaded and rather relieved by what she sees, "How the hell did the cops get there so fast? What really happened back there? Did Mike really shoot at me? Did I even see him?"

Straining to see down the beach, Eliza mutters, "Why the hell are people running that way? What's going on down there?" As she watches, more flashing lights stop along on Shoreline Drive above her home. The image brings a smile to Eliza's face and she mutters, "Look how much higher my home than the others along the Drive. Those lights magnify its difference. What happened down there? Did Mike kill someone?"

When nothing changes after several minutes, the people, that had walked south, slowly trickle back to the north cliffs to blankets and baskets they'd left on the beach. At that time, Eliza decides whatever happened is over and begins the mile walk back to her home. Suddenly, she sees a white car, with lights flashing, speed up Shoreline Drive and turn into the public beach access next to the cliffs. Its lights flash as it weaves its way through the crowds to where she stands. After the patrol car passes her, it stops. Eliza's waits until Frank Gilbert steps out the passenger door and walks back to her.

"You can come home, Eliza. It's over. Mike's gone. Seems he got drunk and bragged he was coming to kill you. The bartender called, so I contacted your Sheriff to watch for him. The county's helicopter flew me over this morning. Deputy Browne got me to your place fast as he could. We knew where Mike was, most of the time, but we couldn't do anything until he made a move on you. The guys saw him drive past your drive early this morning. Must have left his car up the road and doubled back through the dunes.

"Deputy Browne was briefing me when we heard the first shot, then six more. Thank God, he was running when he did and you're a fast mover. He'd a got you, for sure, Eliza. Chased you way into the dunes, all the while, yelling he'd kill you, too, just like Jack and Peg. Deputy Browne hit him in the leg and put him down. Mike yelled, we were too late as he'd killed you. When he tried to reload was when we got him.

"Sorry, I didn't believe you before, Eliza. Hate to tell you, I thought it was you killed Jack. My stupidity near got you killed. Yeah, it was me killed Mike. Wouldn't put down his gun. Brown put another bullet in his leg trying to stop him. But, Mike shot Browne. Nicked his arm. That's when I shot him."

Eliza waits until Frank finishes his story, then she walks away without a word. After she passes the squad car, she runs down the beach to her home. When she reaches her deck, an EMT meets her and takes her down the north deck to a waiting ambulance. There, she's checked over to make certain she has not injuries. Then, the medics pack up and drive the ambulance away.

A minute later, Deputy Browne's patrol car turns down the driveway and stops in front of her garage door. Both Deputy Browne and Frank Gilbert get out and walk up to where she waits. Only the Deputy asks questions and takes a few notes of her answers. When he's finished, he thanks her for her time, wishes her a good day and goes back to the patrol car.

Having stood close to her while she was questioned, Gilbert waits until Deputy Browne turns away. Then he wraps his arms around Eliza in one fast move. Ducking out of his embrace, Eliza pushes him away causing Gilbert to stumble onto the driveway. Looking shocked, he opens his mouth to speak, but Eliza gestures to the patrol car, "Deputy Browne's waiting for you, Frank. Have a good trip home."

TWENTY

Consequences

LIZ turns from the window over her kitchen sink, picks up her mug of coffee and carries it to her dining table to wait for Beth to come back her drive to Hoquium to sign the papers pressing charges against Dee. Thinking over what happened to Beth and herself, Liz wonders if Eliza has faced a trauma as bad as theirs.

As she sips her coffee, Eliza's table adjoins to hers, and she calls out, "Eliza? Are you home? Are you here?" When there's no answer, she sighs. "Poor Eliza, she must have gone to our touchstone and not seeing us there, thinks we're lost to her."

Checking her watch, she sees three hours have passed since the women decided to meet at the north cliffs. "No, if Beth and I went through all we did, Eliza should be back home. Eliza? Are you home?"

"Of course I am, Liz, I was making us sandwiches and brought them over here right after you sat down. I thought you saw me. When I left the house, Mike Hartman ran after me and shot at me. I dodged into the sand dunes and he missed me. I didn't stop until I got to our touchstone. You and Beth weren't there, but I waited for an hour as I was too terrified

167

to go home. Mike had said he would kill me..." Eliza continues telling Liz about the scare she had.

When she finishes, Liz tells what happened to her and then to Beth, "She drove to Hoquium to sign papers at the Sheriff's office to charge her sister for attacking her. I wrote a statement that I had observed the attack. She was lucky. We all were very lucky."

Stunned, Eliza exclaims, "Liz? Don't you see what happened? Bad people came to do each of us harm. Someone tried to kill you. Beth's sister tried to kill her and Mike Hartman tried to kill me. Obviously, what happens to one of us is going to happen to the others. I'm lucky the Sheriff shot and killed Mike as he's closed the book on Jack and Peg's deaths."

Liz gives Eliza a puzzled look, "Eliza, you told Beth and me this morning that you killed your ex and his woman friend. Just because the Sheriff decided it was Mike who did the deed, it doesn't clear your negative karma."

"Yes, Liz, I know you're right." Eliza sighs sadly, "I did what I did and will have to pay somehow. However, that's between you and me and Beth. The Sheriff did me a big favor by killing Mike and declaring the case closed. In many ways that was a lucky shot for me."

Seeing the deep frown on Liz's face, Eliza frowns as she nods. "Yes, yes, I know, I have to find a way to atone for my actions. I'm going to have to do good deeds for the rest of my life as I don't want that load of shit around my neck when I get to the pearly gates. I definitely do not like hot places."

As the two women talk over their experiences, Beth's table adjoins to theirs and she plops down onto one of the chairs. "Hey, what luck to find you both here when I get home. The Sheriff sent a Deputy out looking for Dee. He said he'd call me when they have her in custody but that I should be very cautious until then. I'm hoping today is the last time I have to deal with that horrible bitch. Hi, Eliza, did Liz tell you how close I came to biting the bullet and that she saw my wounds heal? What an amazing thing to happen.

"While I was driving back, Liz, I remembered something else you should know. When I saw the gun in Dee's hand, I turned towards the tables and the two agates were pulsing light. I'd swear that I heard them tell me to lay over the stone. I'd swear they talked to me. That's why I lunged towards the tables after the first bullets ripped through my left arm. I fell then. Must have knocked myself out. After the third shot hit my back. I remember somebody lifting me onto the agate in the floor. Was that you, Liz? I thought it had to be as I felt safe. Must have passed out again then. When I woke, I had healed and you were beside me and told me you saw it happen.

"Finding the agate in the south cliffs and bringing it home was a miracle. The stone told me to place it over the stone in the floor. However, I'm wondering if I would have healed so fast if Liz hadn't been touching me. What do you think?" Beth looks at her others, "Liz? Beth?"

"I don't think I had anything to do with your healing, Beth. When your wounds began to heal, I sat back and only watched. At first, I held your hand and did feel an amazing energy flowing from you. It had to be the energy from the stones which healed your wounds. What else could do it so quickly?"

"Let's try something." Eliza says, "The next time one of us has a cut or injury, no matter how minor, that person should lay on the stones to see what happens. If the injury doesn't heal, we can wait till we're together and try the healing again. It can't do any harm if the injury is small. If it works for us, think of the good we could do with those stones."

Liz puts her hands up and says, "Whoa, gal, let's go slow with this. This healing was Beth's. Not ours. I think it's another sign she is the original Elizabeth Ann Anderson. Whatever it is, Beth obviously has very special connections out there."

Beth laughs, "Okay, ladies, I agree to try the stones' healing properties with our minor injuries. We'll know if it works one way or the other. If the healing doesn't happen, we're off to a doctor's office. However, I don't believe these stones came to us so we can open a clinic of sorts. Nice try, Eliza. However, you're going to have to clean up your own negative karma on your own. I suggest you get busy and look for volunteer work to do. That would do your karma more good than always trying to find the easy way out."

Blushing, Eliza tucks her head and smiles, "Well, a gal can't help trying. When I think of what I've done, it seems that no amount of atonement or good works will ever help."

"Don't try to eat the whole elephant, Eliza. Take a tiny bite at a time. You'll be surprised how much difference you can make in other lives if you take each opportunity that comes to you. Don't worry, once people know you're willing to help, more things will come at you then you'll ever be able to do." Liz tells her.

Beth, seeing the platter of sandwiches Eliza had made, points at them, "Speaking of eating, are those to eat? Good, I'm starving. That drive through Hoquium took me past a great restaurant and the aroma made me realize we should eat together at our adjoined tables as often as we can. It's sure to help strengthen our ties to each other."

"Good idea, Beth. Meeting you two here has been the most important thing I've ever done in many a day. If we meet here after our runs, we'll have time to clean up and fix our lunches. It'll be like having family again. Agreed?"

"Agreed, Eliza. Now you two, hold the rim of the agate bowl and, at the count of three, let's declare our run good and done." Liz says, "One, two..." and at the count of 'three', the Elizabeth Ann Andersons shout, "I declare this run good and done."

CPSIA information can be obtained
at www.ICGtesting.com
Printed in the USA
FSOW02n0455081015
11969FS